WADE'S DANGEROUS DEBUT

Durango Street Theatre – Book 3

Emily Mims

ALSO BY EMILY MIMS

Durango Street Theatre
Vivi's Leading Man
Maggie's Starring Role

The Smoky Blues series
Mist
Smoke
Evergreen
Indigo
Emerald
Mistletoe
Violet
Ruby
Amethyst
Noelle

The Texas Hill Country series
Solomon's Choice
After the Heartbreak
A Gift of Trust
Daughter of Valor
Welcome Home
Unexpected Assets
Never and Always
A Gift of Hope
Once, Again

Other Romances
Season of Enchantment
A Dangerous Attraction
For the Thrill of It All

www.BOROUGHSPUBLISHINGGROUP.com

WADE'S DANGEROUS DEBUT
Copyright © 2019 Emily Wright Mims

ISBN 978-1-951055-36-3

To all the men and women who, for whatever reason, have had to struggle to accept themselves for who they are. We are all beautiful. We need to remember that.

ACKNOWLEDGMENTS

A good book is never written in a vacuum. As always, I owe a debt of gratitude to those who partnered with me on Wade and Owen's story. A warm thanks to everyone at San Antonio's Woodlawn Theater, with special thanks to actor Brian Hodges, who brought both Seymour Krelborn and J. Pierrepont Finch to life on the Woodlawn stage. I'd like to thank beta readers Edwin Floyd, Sharon Middleton, and Troy Bernhardt for their insight and input. Michelle, as always, thanks for a great edit, and a shout-out to the Boroughs Art Department for a fantastic cover. Folks, you are the best.

AUTHOR'S NOTE

Many of my longtime readers will remember Wade Baxter from my Texas Hill Country series. He first appeared as one of Jack Briscoe's football players in *Solomon's Choice*. He appeared again as a college student in *Daughter of Valor,* and *Unexpected Assets,* and was a major supporting character in his mother's story, *Never and Always.* I'm sure those longtime readers are probably thinking, "I didn't know he was gay."

That's all right. Neither did I.

Sometimes characters surprise me like that.

I'm not sure exactly when I began to think about Wade being gay. He was the one character from the Texas Hill Country books whose story was left unresolved at the end of the series. In *Never and Always* his inability to maintain a relationship with a woman is attributed to his negative feelings about his father's family. But what if it was more than that? And how have those unresolved feelings about the Baxters affected him as an adult? Somehow those ideas took hold, and when I decided we needed a gay love story as part of the Durango Street Theater series, it seemed natural to bring Wade back as one of my heroes. It was time for Wade to have his own happily ever after, and it was fun seeing the direction Russ and Angie, and Emily and Jason's lives have taken in the years since their stories were told.

WADE'S DANGEROUS DEBUT

CHAPTER 1

Wade looked down at the specs in his hands, then over at the construction company foreman. The man had a worried frown on his face.

"What do you think, Mr. Baxter? Mr. Klauss asked. "I don't think the expansion joint's wide enough."

"If it's the required inch, then it's fine," Wade said. "You've built it to state specs. We're good."

The foreman breathed a sigh of relief and walked off. Wade wiped the sweat off his forehead. Good old San Antonio, still hot in October. He gazed up at the partially constructed overpass. This update of the busiest highway intersection in Bexar County was going well despite the constant griping of the inconvenienced drivers, the ongoing friction with the construction company representative, and the occasional sniping in the local newspaper's editorial page. They were on schedule and right on budget, and in about a year this spaghetti-like looping of entrances and exits would be serving the lead-footed commuters of San Antonio and its surrounding burgs, who, at that point, would have another huge construction project somewhere else in the city to swear about.

He smiled to himself at the thought. Maybe he would get to head up the next big build himself and not be the second-in-command engineer as he was on this job for the Texas Department of Transportation.

Or maybe not. Only four years out of Texas A&M College of Engineering, he was still a rookie in the DOT pecking order. But he was good at his job, and sooner or later the head engineering spot would go to him.

Not that engineering was what he lived for. Far from it. He glanced down at his watch. Thirty more minutes and it would be quitting time. He hopped into his DOT-issued work truck and drove the half-mile to the field office, a poorly air-conditioned trailer stuffed with too many desks and one old wheezing refrigerator. His grizzled inspector was already seated at his desk going through a pile of paperwork.

"You lighting out early?" he asked Wade.

"Five-thirty-one. You?"

"Five-thirty and a half. The wife's got the car packed already. We're spending the weekend at the ranch. What are you up to this weekend?"

"Oh, this and that," Wade said vaguely. He made it a point not to talk about what he thought of as his "other life" with anyone at work. Not that it was a huge secret. Any of them could easily buy a ticket to one of his performances at the Durango. But so far, none of them had, and if he could keep his two lives separate, he preferred it that way.

Wade tackled his paperwork and had finished when the digital clock turned to the thirty mark. He and his inspector looked at one another and nodded. Considering the long hours they'd put in earlier in the week, Wade didn't feel a bit guilty about packing up and leaving.

He swapped the state vehicle for his own, and cursed as traffic slowed to a crawl. Four years in San Antonio and he still hadn't gotten used to the city's congestion. There wasn't any traffic in the tiny lake community or adjoining small town where he'd grown up, and not that much in College Station. The snarl cost him valuable time getting home for a much-needed shower before heading to the Durango Theatre. Wade's pulse sped up a bit as he whipped into his driveway. Tonight's performance was critical. It was important that he be on top of his game.

He let himself in the front door, and, as always, the stillness struck him as he walked through the quiet rooms. No toys in a basket in the corner. No television turned to SpongeBob or Dora the Explorer. No Sandra rattling around in the kitchen fixing dinner for the three of them. It had been a year since his friend Sandra had moved out and taken her daughter, Noelle, with her, and he still missed them both like a son of a bitch.

Wade sank into the sofa and pulled off his dusty work boots, ran his fingers through his dirty hair, and kicked the boots across the floor. While he missed his former housemates, he could hardly begrudge them their life change. Sandra had reconciled with her estranged husband, Ike, who treated her like a queen and had learned to love Noelle like his own. Ike had made Wade welcome this summer when he'd gone to their home in Tennessee for a visit. Sandra was happier than he'd ever seen her, and Noelle had blossomed in her new environment, acting in plays alongside her mother in the theater Ike and his brothers had bought and renovated.

Wade could never be the husband to Sandra needed. Other than his lovers, she was the only person who'd known the truth about him. No one else knew. Not his family, not his colleagues at work, not even his friends at the Durango. Not that the theater people would care. But that was the way it was going to stay, even if it did make for a lonely existence.

The only real friends he had these days were his colleagues at the Durango. As much as he loved them and shared their joy of performing, often he felt alone in their midst.

Such was the price of secrecy. And he chose to pay it.

The alternative was much too dangerous.

Wade glanced at the clock. Damn, he needed to get moving. He had an important performance to give. He rushed through a shower and shave, and dressed in his signature snap-front shirt and boot-cut jeans. He pulled on the ostrich leather boots his mother had given him for college graduation, and ran a comb through his hair. He nuked a burrito to hold him until later, and left his house.

The traffic had eased up some, and he made good time getting to the Deco District. He parked the F-150 in the lot behind the Durango, and ambled to the back door. This performance and two more, and Seymour Krelborn and *The Little Shop of Horrors* would be history. He could put away the nerdy shopkeeper and his blood-sucking plant and sink his teeth into J. Pierrepont Finch, a character more to his liking. Not that Seymour hadn't been fun. The hapless, lovelorn florist had been a change of pace from the handsome, dashing heroes Wade usually played. But he was ready to bring to life the ambitious window washer in *How to Succeed in Business Without Really Trying*, who follows the advice in a book and becomes chairman of the board.

He looked forward to escaping into the character of J. Pierrepont Finch. And for those two hours being someone else was heaven.

Wade shut the stage door behind him and walked through the storage room of the theater, chock-full of set pieces and props and the odds and ends of theater production. It still smelled of sawdust and fresh paint. Probably would for a few more months. The old movie theater had recently been converted to accommodate live stage productions. The theater was a gift from the gods, purchased by businessman Miguel Abonce for his wife, and they got to use the theater free of charge.

Production costs were another story, but if tonight's special guests, Ernest Navarro and his wife Clarissa, liked what they saw, they might be amenable to awarding a grant to the theater. Executive director Josh Goldstein had told the cast and crew to give it their all.

"Let's show the Navarros what we're made of here at the Durango," their young director extolled them. "Let's put on the performance of a lifetime."

Knowing the cast and crew well, Wade had no doubt they would do exactly that.

Cast members were gathering in the two dressing rooms located behind the stage. He waved as he passed the open door of the ladies' dressing room, where Letti Aldrete was perched on a stool in her underwear while cast-mate Vivienne Abonce wove a head mic through Letti's hair, which would be covered by a blonde wig.

He headed into the men's dressing room, where he shucked his boots, jeans, and shirt. A few minutes at the makeup mirror and his healthy tan was gone, replaced by Seymour's nerdy pallor. Ricardo Pequeño, the older actor playing Mr. Mushnik, helped Wade adjust his face mic and tape the wires that ran down his back to the battery pack that would be concealed by Seymour's baggy khaki pants. Wade donned Seymour's jacket and dorky tennis shoes. Most of the men in the cast were either changing or already in costume. But David York, their deep-throated Audrey II was nowhere to be seen, and his mic was still in its box on the counter.

"Where's David?" Wade asked as he tied his shoelaces.

"Not coming tonight," Duke Duncan, the real-life dentist playing Dr. Scrivello said. "Laryngitis from hell."

"That sucks royally. Especially with the Navarros in the audience. What are we gonna do for an Audrey two?" Wade asked.

"Cameron said not to worry. Somebody named Owen's coming in," Duke answered.

"Who's Owen?" Wade asked.

"Owen? Owen's doing it?" Ricardo's head snapped up. "If Owen's doing it, we have it made in the shade. Chill, Wade, and worry about Seymour."

"If you say so. Where is this Owen?"

"He's on his way." Josh Goldstein stuck his head in the door. "Are we good to go?"

They assured Josh they were ready. The crew chief called out the ten-minute mark, and then five. As Josh stepped on the stage to make his introductions, the backdoor opened and a man slipped into the theater and ducked in the dressing room. Wade looked over his shoulder but caught barely a glimpse of the figure wearing jeans and a hoodie pulled over his head.

Wade picked up the first Audrey II pot plant puppet and took his place for Seymour's first scene. The performance of a lifetime—he could do it. The curtain swept open and something inside him shifted as Wade Baxter faded into the background and Seymour Krelborn took his place. Two lines in and nerdy Seymour had already come to life.

The rest of the cast was as pumped up as he was. The songs and dialogue sparkled. Letti was absolutely rocking Audrey. Duke was knocking it out of the park as the sadistic dentist.

And then Audrey II spoke for the first time. "*Feed me.*"

So much emotion delivered in two simple words. The mesmerizing voice sent chills down Wade's back. Deep, reverberating, captivating, it was a voice any actor would die for. It filled the theater with the perfect touch of velvet menace. Owen, whoever he was, brought the evil plant to life.

Wade's breath caught, but he snapped back into character and delivered Seymour's next lines. He glanced over at the edge of the stage, where Owen stood in the wings. Still wearing the hoodie, the actor had on a face mic and held the manuscript in front of him. The man was taller than average, maybe five-ten or eleven, and had a body to die for: broad shoulders, tight abs, and holy shit, thick powerful thighs. The kind of body Wade loved in a man. He wondered what Owen looked like, but his face remained in shadows. The minute he'd delivered the last of Audrey II's lines, he faded into the background.

Wade was fascinated. Who was this man with the most powerful, seductive voice Wade had ever heard?

He continued to sneak peeks during Audrey II's lines. The minute Dr. Scrivello was consumed and the curtain closed, Wade hustled to the men's dressing room. But the man in a hoodie was nowhere to be seen. Wade didn't dare ask. He didn't want his interest to be obvious.

He didn't want his interest in any man to be obvious.

Intermission ended and he still hadn't caught a glimpse of Owen. But he would have his chance. Rather than waiting in the dressing room between scenes, he stood deep in the wings for the scene between Audrey and Audrey II, and watched as Owen stepped to the edge of the stage, barely out of the audience's view.

Wade felt his dick get hard as Owen's mesmerizing voice filled the auditorium. Owen didn't merely deliver his lines with his voice. He threw his entire body into his delivery, moving in cadence with the puppet on stage, his arms and legs, hips and ass swiveling and dipping and shimmying with each word he spoke. His body was a symphony of motion as he brought Audrey II to life.

He had the grace of a dancer and an uninhibited sensuality that made Wade's mouth water. Wade stared at the man's hard, muscular ass, flexing under the tight jeans as he moved, and Wade sucked in a deep, shuttering breath.

Never more than now, he was thankful for Seymour's baggy, shapeless khakis.

Wade wanted a better look. Even if Owen was straight, he was eye candy of the highest order, and good for a fantasy or two.

The show closed to thunderous applause and a standing ovation. Wade looked around as they took their bows. No Owen. Curious, Wade hot-footed toward the dressing room, but slowed when he spotted Josh and Owen standing deep in the wings.

"Please come out and greet our audience," Josh cajoled. "They would love to meet you."

"Nah, I'd just as soon go on home," Owen said. Without amplification, Owen's voice was softer but no less deep and enthralling. "Here's your mic." He handed Josh the equipment.

"Are you sure?" Josh asked.

"Absolutely."

"Then a million times thank you for saving us tonight."

"My pleasure."

Josh started for the dressing room. Owen turned and the lights from the stage fell across his face. Wade sucked in his breath. One side of Owen's face was sheer perfection—high cheekbone, square jaw, a beautiful brown eye, and warm olive skin.

The other side of his face was a crazy quilt of red, raised scar tissue, and an eye that had to be fake.

Wade stared in shock at the mottled scarring. Owen raised his gaze and met Wade's for a moment before turning his head and walking away.

***

The hottie playing Seymour hadn't been shy about checking him out.

And he hadn't been able to hide his shock at the devastation Owen called a face these days.

Owen skirted the edge of the stage and walked past the empty dressing rooms, glad the cast was headed to the lobby for the traditional meet and greet. The last thing he wanted to do this evening was endure the pitying looks of his old friends, or the horror on the faces in the Durango crowd he didn't know. Most of all, he wasn't in the mood to face the tight-mouthed displeasure of his ex-wife. The only thing he wanted this evening was to get back to his apartment as quickly as he could and cocoon himself in the solitude he craved like a drug. He worried he was in danger of turning into a recluse, but the alternative posed more complications than he thought he could stand.

He hadn't wanted to come this evening, but his old friend, Cameron Heiser, the current chairman of the Durango board, had called and begged him.

"Josh or I can do it if we have to. But nobody has a voice like yours. We have a major potential benefactor and his wife coming tonight and we really, really need to impress them."

So Owen had sucked it up and went as a favor to Cameron.

Owen had heard from his daughter, Sophie, that the theater was hurting financially, and the last thing he wanted was for the theater that meant so much to his daughter and her mother, and had once meant so much to him, to go down. So he'd agreed, and spent part of the afternoon going through the manuscript and practicing instead of working on the webpage he was updating for the San Antonio Police

Department. He would have to pull an all-nighter or get up at butt-crack thirty to get the damned thing finished by Monday.

It hurt walking out of this new and improved Durango Theatre. His son Marco hadn't been interested, but his daughter Sophie had kept him apprised of the drama surrounding the loss of the old theater and the acquisition of the new one.

Owen stopped a minute to breathe in the aroma of fresh wood and paint and the giddy optimism he felt from the cast and crew tonight. They had all been crushed at the loss of the old downtown Durango, and elated when Miguel Abonce purchased this new one for his wife. And Abonce had spared no expense on the conversion. It was every amateur company's dream theater. Exactly what Owen would have ordered up if he'd been in charge.

If things had been different, it was where he would still be acting today.

Pincers of regret wrapped around Owen's heart and squeezed. No way was he ever going to tread the boards again, belt out a Broadway show tune, or deliver a killer knockout line to an eager audience.

No way was he going to take his bows or shake hands in the lobby with audience members gushing over his performance and maybe flirting with him. His acting days were over. His career with the San Antonio Police Department was over. His marriage to Letti was sure as hell over. His old life, the one he'd lived up until five years ago, was gone, never to return.

Sometimes it felt like his whole life was over.

He held back the morbid and remembered his blessings. He still had his children. He had a new career. His webpage design business wasn't all that lucrative, at least not yet, but between his disability pension and his IT business, he paid the bills, and his ex, Letti, got a healthy child support check each month.

And he had embraced the new direction his life had taken since he'd decided to stop pretending to be someone he wasn't and to be honest with the world. He was gay. He didn't care who knew it. He was proud of who he was. And he had damn little patience for gay folks who weren't.

The world was way past Stonewall and 1969.

He let himself out of the theater and clicked open his Mazda CX-5. His thoughts drifted back to the good-looking young actor playing

Seymour. Wade something or another. The man was a hottie. No other word for it. Bigger than most stage actors, the guy had to top six feet by two or three inches. Square face, high, defined cheekbones, expressive, whiskey-colored eyes, sculpted lips, and a chin and jawline that had come straight out of Hollywood casting. Unruly brown hair that Owen longed to touch had stuck out from under Seymour's cap.

Unfortunately, Seymour's baggy clothes had concealed most of Wade's body, but Owen had seen the outline of a solid, well-muscled chest, broad shoulders, narrow hips, and powerful thighs. He couldn't be sure what Wade's speaking voice sounded like since he'd heard him only as the nerdy Seymour, but his singing voice was a rich, vibrant tenor that reverberated through the theater.

Oh, yeah. Wade was one fine piece of man candy.

Too bad he'd never be interested in a scarred, broken-down man like Owen.

No point bemoaning something that would never be. Owen firmed his lips and pulled out of the parking lot. This late in the evening traffic was non-existent, and he sped overland toward the two-bedroom apartment he called home these days.

His favorite drive-thru taco place was still open, so he detoured around the building and ordered a bulging sack of *carne guisada* and bean and cheese tacos, figuring what he didn't eat for supper he could nuke and eat the next day. He pulled into his parking slot, eager to sit and feast on the tacos, and groaned when he spotted the lights on behind his curtains and a familiar old Honda parked three cars down.

The last thing he wanted this evening was to deal with his fresh-faced, bubbly, cheerfully optimistic seventeen year-old. He'd much rather a sharp-tongued, bitter exchange with her mother. That would've fit his mood perfectly.

Sophie was here, and he'd be damned if he'd be a shit to her. It wasn't her fault he was in a foul mood. It wasn't her fault he'd lost his law enforcement career trying to defuse a bomb. It wasn't her fault he and her mother had divorced bitterly. It wasn't her fault he was missing singing and acting like a son of a bitch. His girl deserved a sweet, loving father who was glad to see her. And that was what she was going to get.

He bounded up the stairs two at a time and threw open the door. "To what do I owe the pleasure of a visit from my favorite princess?"

"Daddy." Sophie jumped off the sofa and smothered him in a huge hug, then tilted her head back. "You brought food. Is there enough for me?"

"Yes, princess, there's plenty." Owen returned his daughter's exuberant embrace. "Good week at school?"

"The best." She released him and took the bag of tacos from his hands. "The engineering club designed a robot we think has a chance to win State, and our *Little Shop* rehearsals went great. Jessica said I was as good an Audrey as Mom."

"I'm sure she's right. Grab sodas and plates and we'll eat."

They sat across from one another and unwrapped a taco each, leaving the rest in the bag to stay warm. Owen opened the hot sauce and poured it liberally into his taco.

"That's gonna give you heartburn, Daddy."

Owen grinned, ignoring the way the smile pulled at his scars. "It'll be worth it. So what brings you my direction tonight? I'd think you'd be on a date or out with your Durango buddies."

"They all had to go home early. Our production's tomorrow afternoon, and their moms insisted they get a good night's sleep."

Owen raised his eyebrow. "And your mom didn't?"

"Course she did. But I told her I wouldn't stay long." She looked at him thoughtfully. "You didn't come out and shake hands. You should have. I heard Mr. Navarro tell Mr. Summerset you had an awesome voice and that he really wanted to meet you. He said he wanted to put a face with the voice."

"And that, princess, is exactly why I didn't." He reached out when Sophie's face fell. "Honey, don't look at me like that. Don't you think I wish I could go out and meet the audience again? I'd love to get back up on that stage and sing and dance again."

"I know you do." She studied his face for a minute, a long, uncomfortable minute that had Owen wanting to throw up his hands and hide his scars. "Your face isn't that bad, Daddy. Really. And the marks on your arm and hand are nothing."

"Sorry, baby girl, but it is that bad. My face is, anyway. The guy playing Seymour got a good look at me and couldn't hide his horror. And I heard he's a good actor."

"I'm guessing it took Wade by surprise," Sophie insisted. "I doubt he was horrified. Wade's a nice guy, as nice as they come. He wouldn't be all that upset by a few scars."

"If you say so." He wasn't going to argue with her. He knew horror when he saw it, and Wade had been horrified.

"I say so. I know him pretty well. He's been in a bunch of shows, and he's been really nice about helping out with the kids in the Academy."

"Does he usually play romantic leads?"

Sophie nodded. "Nearly always. With a face and a voice like that, he's a natural at that kind of role."

Owen bit his lip. It was on the tip of his tongue to ask more. But he didn't want his too-savvy daughter to guess his interest in the guy.

"So are you ready to best your mother's performance tomorrow?" he deflected.

"Yep. I am." Her smile was cheeky. "Even if she won't admit it. You know how Mom is about her acting."

Owen tried not to grimace in front of his daughter. From the nearly twelve years he'd spent married to Letti, he knew all too well how she was about her acting. At the same time, she was the stage mother from hell and was more than ready to sing her daughter's praises.

"Your mom will be delighted that you do well," he told his girl.

"Well, Mom's not the point. I came over to make sure you're planning to come. I got you a ticket in the third row." She fished a ticket out of her pocket.

"Princess, no. Not the third row."

Sophie's eyes flashed. "Worried somebody might see you?"

"Something like that. It hurts, princess, when people stare."

Sophie's expression softened. "I know you hate the stares, but how else are you going to see me? Are you going to stay home like you did last time and watch Mr. Harris's video on Flickr? That blows."

She pushed the ticket across the table. "This is next to Mom, *Abuelita*, and *Bisabuela* if she's up to it. Please, Daddy. You came for Mr. Heiser tonight. You can come for me tomorrow." She giggled. "Besides, it'll be fun to watch *Abuelita* swell up like a toad when you sit next to her. She'll purse her lips like this," she screwed her lips up in a perfect imitation of her grandmother's scowl, "and cross herself." She clicked her tongue and made her grandmother's sign of the cross. "She told Mom she prays for you every night. Mom asked if she was praying for your favorite gay bar to burn down. *Abuelita* didn't think Mom was funny."

After he'd come out, his son and daughter had taken the news in stride. The older generation, not so much.

Make that not at all.

Owen couldn't help it. He laughed out loud at Sophie. "Okay, I'll come. If for no other reason than to piss off your grandmother." Not that he was looking forward to sitting with Team Letti. Even if Sophie thought it was funny.

She jumped up and threw her arms around his neck. "Thanks, Daddy. It means a lot."

Thirty minutes and three tacos later, she was gone. Owen's eyes were hooded as he stood on his front porch and watched her drive away. She didn't think he looked that bad. That's a daughter for you. But he knew better. The stares, the gasps, and the rapidly averted glances...he'd seen the reactions of strangers too often to believe her. He should be used to it by now, but over the years it had gotten more painful to bear, not less.

Ultimately, it was easier to stay home.

He went back inside and shut the door. He took a minute to survey the cozy nest he lived in. Unlike most bachelor pads, his reflected the time and care he had put into decorating it with the stylish leather furniture from his former man-cave at Letti's house, a small but beautiful oak dining table, and pictures and keepsakes on bookshelves flanking the wall-mounted television. He'd set up one workstation in the living room and a second in the guest bedroom that doubled as a place for his kids to crash when they spent time with him. He'd fixed up that room as well as his bedroom, turning the stark, impersonal apartment into a comfortable place to live, to work, and to hang out.

To hide.

Owen shrugged. If that was the case, then so be it. He switched on the living room computer and made a cup of coffee while the machine's hard drive made its usual startup whistles and chirps. If Sophie expected him to attend her performance, he was losing his work time tomorrow. He would have to get as far as possible on the SAPD website update tonight.

As he sat in front of the computer, with his coffee, he wondered briefly if Wade would be there tomorrow afternoon. Sophie had said, and Owen knew, most of the adult performers took an interest in the Academy kids and would most likely be there to support them.

The odds were good that he'd see the hottie again tomorrow.

Not that the hottie would have one bit of interest in him.

CHAPTER 2

Wade smiled as he shook Byron Summerset's hand.

"Great show. Y'all knocked it out of the ballpark," Byron gushed.

"F-f-fantastic," his wife Barbara added. "Y-you were w-wonderful."

Wade leaned down and kissed Barbara gently on the cheek. "I take that as high praise. Especially from the mom of an up-and-coming Hollywood star."

Barbara blushed prettily. "T-thanks."

"More importantly, you and your fellow cast-mates impressed the hell out of Ernest and Clarissa," Byron said. "I saw him round up your executive director and artistic director and hustle them off. I promise you, a check is being written as we speak."

"Which will have us all breathing a sigh of relief," Wade said. "Even with us acting free, it costs money to keep a place like this going. We've certainly appreciated your support over the years."

"It's our pleasure."

As the Summersets moved on to shake hands with the next actor, Wade peered down the line of well-wishers. Just a few more handshakes and he could get out of costume and either head for the house or down two blocks to Thirties, the noisy bar and grille the theater crowd discovered shortly after the *Little Shop* run began. Right now was a toss-up. He had no desire to go home to an empty house, but he didn't have any desire to make idle small talk in a bar.

Or to be hit on by a woman he would have to turn down.

Or get hit on by a man he'd like to go home with, which he would *never* do in front of the Durango crowd.

He would decide after he'd changed clothes and washed off all the stage makeup.

And asked a few questions about the mysterious Owen.

Dutifully, he shook hands with the remaining patrons and fended off a teasing pass from one of their season ticket holders who promised him that sooner or later he'd cave and go out with her. He stifled a grin as she went on down the line. Not his type, even if he'd been straight. Finally, he got to the last patron and breathed a sigh of relief. "Come on," he said to Letti, who'd been standing next to him. "Let's get out of these costumes and hit the bar."

"Out of costume, you bet." She looked at the green satin jumpsuits they all wore for the last scene. "Not sure about the bar, though. Sophie's due home in a little while, and I need to make sure she doesn't sit up until the wee hours playing Besiege. She has a performance tomorrow and needs to be fresh."

"I play that. Puts my degree to use a little."

Letti laughed. "She plays fine without an engineering degree."

"It certainly went well tonight," he said sotto voce. "Owen sure saved our butts. We owe him a big one."

Letti's lips tightened. "So what if we do? This theater does plenty for his own. It didn't hurt him to give back a little tonight."

Wade turned to look at her. "The theater does plenty for his own what?"

"His kids. My kids. Sophie and Marco. The theater's turned itself inside out for the asshole's children when he wouldn't anymore. So no, it didn't hurt the SOB to get his butt in here and help us tonight."

"I'm still grateful," Wade said cautiously. Owen was her ex? He tamped down his disappointment. If Owen had been married, most likely, he was straight.

"Knock yourself out. I'm not going to bother." Letti stomped toward the women's dressing room.

Shit. He'd stepped in a cow turd, big time.

Puzzled, he ambled toward the men's dressing room. Ricardo was unhooking Duke's mic, and a couple of the ensemble players were changing into their street clothes.

"So, you think we impressed the bigwigs tonight?" Ricardo asked as he handed Duke the mic and power box.

"Mr. Summerset said we did. Apparently, he talked to the Navarros during intermission. He said they corralled Josh and Rachel after the show and spirited them away. I'm hoping they give us money." Wade sat and pulled off the tennis shoes.

One of the ensemble helped him get out of the green satin jumpsuit, and Ricardo carefully removed the head mic.

"If we do get something tonight, we have Owen to thank for some of it." Ricardo handed the mic to Wade.

"Letti doesn't think so," Wade said.

"Oh, hell. You didn't say something nice about Owen to that woman, did you?" Ricardo whistled under his breath. "Jesus, why would you do a thing like that? Now she'll be pissed at you for weeks."

"What did I do? It was nice of him to help out at the last minute. We owe him." He pulled on his jeans and rubbed a cotton pad soaked with makeup remover over the pale stage makeup.

Ricardo shook his head. "Never mind."

Wade opened his mouth to ask another question, but Josh burst into the dressing room with a huge smile on his face.

"You impressed the hell out of the Navarros tonight."

"That's good." Wade pushed Josh down on a stool. "Tell us how impressed."

"Three hundred thousand impressed."

"Three hundred thousand?" Wade sputtered.

"You heard me," Josh said.

"Over how long?" Duke asked. "Two years? Three?"

"Like, *tonight*."

Wade dropped his boot on the floor. "You mean he wrote you a check for three hundred grand tonight? Yee-haw." He punched his fist in the air.

The men broke into cheers and high-fives. Josh accepted the congratulations and promised to buy the first round of drinks before heading to the women's dressing room to deliver the same news. In a moment a commotion started up in the other dressing room.

"Sounds like the ladies are as happy as we are," Ricardo said.

"Lots of reason to be happy. So, are you taking Josh up on his offer of a drink?" Wade asked Ricardo.

"Nah. I'm on grandkid duty in the morning. My daughter has a Saturday morning class."

Damn. There went his chance to find out anything more about Owen. Or at least find out why Letti was so pissed with her ex. Maybe someone else would know. Surely someone would be willing to indulge in a little gossip.

The jubilant Durango crowd had already commandeered a corner of the bar by the time he walked in the door. Josh must have made a phone call or two. Besides the *Little Shop* cast and crew, Vivienne's husband Miguel had joined them. Cameron Heiser and a couple of other board members were also in attendance.

Vivienne motioned him over to the booth where she was sitting with Miguel and Cameron. Wade shook hands with the men and exchanged a high-five with Vivienne before sliding in beside Cameron, careful not to sit too close. "Good night, isn't it?"

"I'll say. A crap-pile of worry off my mind." As chairman of the board, Cameron was responsible for everything Durango and kept his eye on the bottom line. The Navarros' generosity went a long way toward making his job a whole lot easier.

"Makes me happy our investment isn't coming to naught." Miguel kissed Vivienne's cheek.

"Makes me happy all I have to worry about is my next performance," Vivienne said. "And the load of steel that's a week late." She and her brother Cameron ran a steel fabrication company that had been in the family for five generations. Wade started to make a joke about San Antonio royalty, but the last time he'd done that, Vivi had taken great pleasure in reminding him of his own noble connections, as a grandson of the illustrious Harrington-Riley clan.

Better to introduce the topic of Owen instead, if he could figure out how without revealing his interest.

Vivienne looked around at the revelers in their corner. "I don't see Letti. I thought surely she would come tonight."

Oh, Vivi, thank you. "She said she was going home to make sure Sophie got a good night's sleep. And that was before I pissed her off royally."

"How'd you do that?"

"I said we owe Owen for coming in tonight. Got under her skin big-time."

His statement was met with groans.

"You blew it, man," Cameron said. "As far as Letti's concerned, Owen's picture is beside weasel, rat, snake, and asshole in the dictionary. And a few more besides. She's been royally pissed at him and has been since their breakup."

"How long ago was the divorce?" Wade asked.

Vivienne thought a minute. "Gosh, I guess it's been five years now."

"Five years," Miguel confirmed. "You and I had started seeing one another when their divorce was near final. You entertained me with the story for months." He turned to Wade. "It was my introduction to the behind-the-scenes drama in the theater world."

"What drama?" Wade asked. "And was it before or after whatever happened to his face?"

"During, actually," Cameron said. "Letti and Owen were acting in *White Christmas* with Johnny and Beth Roberts. Everything was going fine, and then it wasn't. Letti kicked Owen out of the house, screaming he was having an affair with Beth, even though Beth swore it wasn't true. Letti said she'd seen his car parked next to Beth's in a motel parking lot. They were in the middle of the divorce from hell when he got hurt and Jessica's husband, Robby, got killed trying to defuse a bomb."

"Owen's a cop?" Wade asked.

"Was." Vivienne picked up the story. "Besides pretty much devastating his face, it cost him his left eye. He got a disability retirement. The city declared him a hero and pinned all kinds of medals on him. Didn't make a whit of difference to Letti. She went right on with the divorce and has been royally pissed ever since."

"Especially when Owen came out of the closet," Miguel added.

Out of the closet? Wade's heart skipped a beat. "He's gay?"

"He never made any kind of announcement or anything like that," Cameron said, "or been particularly public about it, but Letti's made a few cracks about him batting for the other team. And Josh saw him in a gay bar."

"But the real kicker came the following year when Johnny and Beth got a divorce and Johnny also came out of the closet. "Waaay out of the closet." Vivienne giggled. "It seems that Owen was having the affair with Johnny, not Beth."

"And Letti blames Owen for everything. Never mind that she was rumored to be carrying on too," Cameron stated.

"The whole thing's a crying shame." Vivienne shook her head. "Owen's a nice guy, as nice as they come. Maybe not the brightest when it came to how he conducted his love life, but hardly the monster Letti makes him out to be."

"Amen to that," Cameron murmured.

"Fascinating story." Wade couldn't believe what he'd learned. The waitress brought their drinks, and he picked up his longneck and drank deeply. "Is she still angry with him over the affair? Tonight she said something about the theater doing for his kids when he wouldn't."

"He used to be a real hands-on parent. Volunteered with the Academy, coached Marco's Little League team, the whole nine yards," Cameron said. "Now he stays holed up in his apartment all the time. Wouldn't even come to Sophie's last play. I'm guessing Letti thinks he's dropped the ball where the kids are concerned."

"Any idea why he won't do more?" Wade turned his bottle around in his hands.

"I think he's self-conscious about his face," Vivienne said softly. "The few times I've seen him since the accident, he's tried to hide it. A ball cap, a cowboy hat, sunglasses, a hoodie... He dresses to conceal the imperfections." She sipped her wine. "It's a shame about the scarring. He was so good-looking before. And so talented. You heard his speaking voice. Now imagine him singing 'They Call the Wind Mariah' in that voice of his. He could dance really well, too."

"So why doesn't he sing and dance? He doesn't look all that bad." Wade drank another pull of beer. "Not so bad that he needs to hide out from the world. One of my college roommates was burned badly in Iraq. Jason has no face left. No ears, no hair, no nothing. And he sells cars. Successfully."

"Sounds like your friend's scars are all on the outside," Miguel noted. "Maybe Owen's run deeper."

Scars on the inside. The thought drew Wade up short. Of all people, he could identify with that.

The conversation drifted to a discussion of the upcoming production. Wade listened with half an ear. He couldn't get Owen Aldrete off his mind. A genuine hero injured trying to defuse a bomb, yet a wounded man hiding out from the world, and a talented man letting his gifts go unused.

A man brave enough to come out of the closet and live the life he was meant to.

A man Wade would like to meet.

And maybe get to know a whole lot better.

He would be the perfect boyfriend, Wade thought later as he listened to rain pepper his roof. He relaxed on his sofa as he sipped another beer and flipped through the after-midnight offerings on cable. Great body, great voice. They shared a love for theater. And although Owen was out of the closet, he didn't like to be seen in public. They could see one another behind closed doors. They could keep their relationship private. He could stay out of the gay bars, where he was always looking over his shoulder.

It sounded better than meeting new men online, which was the way he'd been doing it for the last five years.

Owen Aldrete would be the perfect boyfriend for him.

***

Owen ignored the warning sign about being towed, and parked his car in front of a small dry-cleaners halfway down the block from the Durango. The sun shone brightly and the air was cool and crisp, thanks to the mild norther that had moved through last night and dumped an inch of rain on the parched city.

Before the accident, he would have enjoyed spending an afternoon like this out in the sunshine, but his scars were bad enough without aggravating them with a sunburn. He wasted no time getting to the theater. The doors were unlocked, and with nearly an hour before the performance, the lobby was deserted.

He took a minute to take in the fresh paint and carpet. It looked a lot like the old Durango, which didn't surprise him. According to his daughter, this theater and the old Durango had shared an architect and a builder. This one predated the downtown theater by a few years and looked like something out of a '40s noir movie. He ran his hand across the concession stand bar. Vintage elegant, with a bit of funky thrown in.

A fierce wave of longing washed over him as he wandered deeper into the lobby, the deco chandeliers casting a gentle light on the deep scarlet carpets. He should have been part of the new theater. He should be up on that stage, singing and dancing his heart out. Instead, a cruel twist of fate had relegated him to live the rest of his life in the shadows, hiding his pitiful excuse for a face from the world.

The front doors opened and a mother and her two children stepped inside. Owen fingered the ticket in his pocket. He turned to walk into the theater but couldn't make himself take the steps. The ticket was for a chair in the third row. He would be visible to the rest of the audience and every kid up on the stage. There would be shock and stares, and the inevitable, "Mommy, what's wrong with his face?" Or worse, the quickly averted stares.

He couldn't face it. Not even for Sophie.

Surely there was a less conspicuous place where he could sit and watch his daughter's performance. He glanced around the lobby and spotted a cordoned-off staircase that probably led to a balcony. Slipping around the velvet piping, he ran up the stairs two at a time. The smell of paint and carpet cleaner assaulted him as he reached the top of the stairs and stepped into a smaller version of the downstairs lobby.

Stacks of boxes lined the freshly painted walls, and sixties-era costumes hung from a portable clothing rack. He stepped onto the balcony, avoiding the sound boxes where the musicians played for the adult performances. This afternoon the music would be canned and managed from the soundboard in the back of the theater downstairs.

Unless there were others who also wished to remain unseen, he would have the balcony to himself.

He sat in the third row and propped his feet on the chair in front of him, yawning widely as the almost all-nighter he'd pulled started to catch up with him. At least he'd be able to get some sleep tonight and maybe enjoy a steamy dream or two about going after it with the hottie, Wade. Not for the first time today, he wondered if Sophie was right, that Wade was interested in the Academy kids and would come see the performance this afternoon.

He watched with wistful emotions as the theater slowly filled with friends and family of the young actors. When he'd performed, he'd loved peeking from the wings as the theater filled up. And today it would be full, or close to it. Jessica Clary, the Academy director, worked miracles with the kids, and the teen productions were often as good as the adult performances. Despite their antagonism, he'd admired the performance his ex-wife put on last night, and had no doubt his daughter's would be equally as wonderful.

Jessica and Josh made the usual introductions. The curtain swept open and Owen was instantly transported into the story. Within five minutes, he could tell this afternoon's performance was going to be exceptional. Sophie's performance was everything Letti's had been last night.

The play finished to rousing applause and flowers for Sophie. He sat patiently waiting for the theater to clear before he made his escape. He had no desire to face the stares from strangers or the glares from Team Letti. He would call Sophie on the way home and tell her how well she did and how proud he was of her.

The theater was almost empty when he heard movement behind him and turned to find his ex-wife stomping down the balcony stairs.

"What the hell are you doing up here?" she demanded. "You had a ticket for the third row."

"It's more enjoyable to watch my daughter without the laser glares from Team Letti blinding my vision."

"Guess you better not come downstairs, then. The tears in your daughter's eyes might blind you." She shot daggers at him. "She thinks you didn't come and she's about to cry."

"Aw, hell." Owen jumped out of his chair. "I told her I'd be here."

"Your chair was empty and you missed the last one. What's she supposed to think?"

Sophie probably thought he'd stood her up.

Owen loped down the stairs with Letti on his heels. The crowd in the lobby had mostly thinned with only a few of the parents and teens milling about. Sophie's smile morphed from forced to genuine when she spotted him.

"Daddy, where were you? I thought you hadn't come." She threw her arms around his neck for a huge hug.

Owen felt tears prick the back of his eyelids. "I told you I'd be here, princess. And you were wonderful." He shot a look at Letti.

For once, his ex-wife could be gracious.

"She was, wasn't she?" Letti's face beamed with pride.

"Yes, our Sophia was wonderful. Absolutely wonderful." Carmela Lopez curled her lip as she looked at him.

His former mother-in-law had never been a fan, and what little regard she'd had for him evaporated when he came out of the closet.

Nevertheless, he turned and smiled at her and Letti's birdlike grandmother, who was also giving him the stink eye.

"How are you ladies this afternoon?" he asked pleasantly, offering his hand.

The last thing either of them wanted to do was to shake, but it was either that or make a scene, so they nodded regally and shook his hand reluctantly. They quickly stepped away, lest they be drawn into conversation and have to be polite to him in front of others.

The line of patrons moved along and Owen found himself greeting the rest of the cast, trying not to flinch when they spotted his face and reacted. He was almost to the end of the line when Wade came around the corner carrying a box of popcorn in each hand. Owen's breath caught in his throat. Despite the Seymour Krelborn costume and makeup last night, Wade had been yummy. This afternoon, dressed in jeans that left little to the imagination, and a snap-front western shirt that emphasized his broad shoulders and powerful chest, the man was sex on a stick. Owen felt himself start to harden as Wade grinned impudently at someone across the room. It was all he could do to keep his eyes pointing forward and not watch Wade's sexy swagger as he crossed the lobby while thinking he'd love to meet the man, but couldn't take the guaranteed rejection.

He shook hands with the last two cast members and went to where Sophie was standing with Wade and a couple of the street singers from the play. Wade was laughing and talking to the girls.

Sophie turned to Owen with a big smile on her face. "Daddy, this is Wade Baxter. He played Seymour last night, remember?"

"I remember well." He turned to Wade, dreading the inevitable upcoming wince, and offered his hand. "Owen Aldrete. Audrey II when the occasion warrants. Proud father of Sophie."

"Wade Baxter. Proud mentor of these young ladies, and Seymour when the occasion warrants. I didn't see you in the audience."

A shiver ran down Owen's back. Wade's speaking voice was as beautiful as his singing voice. Owen pointed up. "I watched from the balcony." He stuck out his hand.

Wade fumbled with the popcorn box in his right hand, finally handing it to Sophie. He took Owen's hand in a grip that made his fingers tingle, and he felt himself tremble. Did Wade feel that?

If he did, he gave no sign of it. He shook Owen's hand and graced him with a friendly but reserved smile. "You have every right to be proud. Sophie knocked it out of the ballpark." He turned to the other girls. "And Lacey and Giselle did wonderful jobs this afternoon too."

"Yes, they did." Owen had already shaken the girls' hands and ignored their winces.

Wade turned back to Owen, his expression friendly but devoid of any awareness or interest. "We owe you a debt of gratitude for last night. The Navarros were impressed. They bestowed generously."

"I doubt I had much to do with it. You all put on an amazing performance." Owen was at a loss. Last night, he could have sworn Wade was checking him out. But this afternoon, the man displayed no more interest in him than any straight man would, and he was beginning to ask himself if Wade's interest in him last night had been a figment of his imagination.

Maybe Wade was straight after all.

What a disappointment that would be.

Owen's gaze met Wade's for the smallest fraction of a second. There it was, the tiniest flare of interest before Wade tamped it back down with an expression of friendly neutrality. So Wade was gay, but he was hiding it, revealing his interest subtly, and only another gay man would pick up on it.

The good-looking young man wasn't out of the closet.

Damn. That sucked big-time. Owen felt a surge of anger. Another gay man ashamed of who he was. He choked back his disappointment. If Wade wasn't out at the theater where nobody would care about his sexual preference, he wasn't out period, and surely not looking for a boyfriend who made no bones about who he was.

Not that the hunk would be interested in him, anyway. Wade couldn't be much over twenty-five or twenty-six, and as handsome as sin. He wasn't going to be interested in a boyfriend who'd left forty behind in the rearview a year ago and had a face out of a horror film. Still, it would have been fun to have him as a friend. If Wade wasn't out, he wasn't going to want to hang out with others who were.

Wade handed the second box of popcorn to Giselle. "You girls enjoy." The teenagers dug into their popcorn.

Letti and her mother approached the group. "We're going to that pizza place down the street. Wade, would you like to come with?" She turned reluctantly toward her ex. "Owen?"

"Daddy, can you come?" Sophie added eagerly. "And Wade."

Owen held his breath. If Wade was going, it might be worth the stares in the pizza parlor for a chance to get to know the guy a little.

Wade shook his head. "I already promised Bobby Clary that his mom and I would take him to Chuck E. Cheese's."

Owen felt himself deflate even further. If Wade was taking out women, he was seriously in the closet. Even if he were interested in Owen, he wouldn't act on it.

"Okay. Give Bobby a hug for me." She turned to Owen. "Daddy?"

"Princess, I wish. But I have at least eight more hours of work on a project that's due in the morning." And he wouldn't have to suffer through Team Letti and the stares all evening.

Sophie's face fell. "Maybe next time," she said quietly.

Letti's lip curled and she shot him a look of disgust. *Coward,* she mouthed.

He ignored his ex and turned to his daughter. "Call me tomorrow or the next day. There's a traveling exhibition of Broadway costumes at the museum. We can go next Saturday afternoon, if you like."

"I like." Sophie perked up and Owen felt relieved.

As they left the theater, Wade passed Owen and handed him a folded program.

"Here. You didn't get one sitting upstairs."

"Thanks." Owen took the program.

Wade veered off toward a side parking lot at the end of the block, and Owen found his car ticketless in front of the dry cleaners. It had warmed up some during the afternoon, so he lowered the windows and ran the A/C on high for a moment. He glanced down at a less elaborate version of the adult program and started to flip to Sophie's bio when he noticed writing across the top of the cast photo. He looked closer and sucked in his breath. A phone number with a hill country area code and Wade's email address were printed above the picture.

His fingers holding the program started to tremble. The hottie had reached out to him. Despite the age difference. Despite his scars. Owen's face split into a wide smile that pulled on his scars. Wade Baxter had made the first move.

Now it was up to Owen to make the next one.

CHAPTER 3

Wade threw his dusty hardhat on the sofa and flopped down beside it. The cool snap from the weekend was long gone, and the hot sun had baked him all afternoon on the job site. He was bone tired and thankful there was no scheduled rehearsal tonight. He could throw a steak in the pan and eat a bagged salad and chill.

And wonder why Owen Aldrete hadn't gotten back to him yet.

God, he hoped he hadn't misread the situation. He could have sworn the guy was checking him out the other day. And Vivienne and Cameron said he had come out. But what if they were wrong?

Or worse, Owen wasn't interested in him.

Either way, he hoped to hell the man hadn't said anything to anyone else.

He wandered into the bathroom and stripped. His shower stall was small, but the water pressure was strong, pulsing across his back and shoulders while the dust and dirt sluiced off him and down the drain. He toweled off with one of the thick towels Sandra had bought, and pulled on a pair of cutoffs from his college days.

He glanced out at the grill. Nah, too much trouble for one steak. He melted a pat of butter in his mother's old cast-iron skillet and was about to drop in the sirloin when his phone rang. Wade's heart leapt. Maybe it was Owen. He looked down at the screen and stifled a groan. Emily Donahue, his old friend from College Station, who'd lived next door, and married one of his roommates. She and her husband were two of his best friends in the world, and he loved them both dearly. But she was the last person he wanted to talk to right now.

He would bet his next paycheck Emily had found another woman to introduce to him.

She meant well. God bless her. Since Sandra moved out, Emily had made it her mission in life to find him a new girlfriend, calling every month or two with another name and phone number, delivered with peppy enthusiasm and a sincere, "I think you'd really like her."

He might, but not the way Emily thought he would.

He would have to make excuses yet again.

He started to let it go to voicemail, but then Emily would get worried. So he turned off the burner and answered.

"Yo, Emily, what's up? How are the monsters?"

"We had a pee fight in the front bathroom this morning. Jace showed Riley how to aim. Quite the mess."

"They had a pee fight in that fancy front bathroom? The white one?" Wade laughed out loud.

"Yep. I thought Jason was going to split his sides laughing. Right in front of them."

He could hear her exasperation.

"The SOB had the gall to be proud."

"Men always are. The things I missed, growing up an only child."

They spent the requisite few minutes catching up on gossip. Then Emily got to it, mentioning a colleague in her doctoral program.

"Heather's pretty, sweet, and sharp as a tack. She grew up in Crockett and plays three musical instruments. Sings some, too. I think you'd really like her!"

Here we go again. "Honestly, Emily, I probably would if I had time to take her out. But between the job and all the rehearsals, I don't have time to do my laundry, much less take a lady on a date."

"What rehearsals? You finished a production, like, yesterday."

"And I landed the lead in the new one. We're doing *How to Succeed in Business Without Really Trying,* and I got the J. Pierrepont Finch role. So I don't have time for a social life."

He could feel Emily deflate.

"Okay. But you have to start dating sometime. I know you were broken up over Sandra, but it's been a year since she left. You need to get out there and start dating other people. Someday, you're going to want to get married and have a family. And to do that you have to meet someone."

No, he wouldn't want to get married and have a family. He would have loved a child. But closeted gay men didn't get to be fathers. Not without announcing their status to the world.

Emily went on in the same vein for a few minutes, before she excused herself to fix dinner for her kids.

He rewarmed the skillet and threw in the steak, his mouth watering at the tantalizing sizzle. He felt a little guilty, letting her think he was broken up over Sandra. Emily had presumed, as had everyone else, that he and Sandra had been a couple. It suited them to let people think that. She was the perfect beard, and had her own reasons for perpetrating the lie. But now she was gone. Sooner or later, Emily and Jason and everyone else were going to wonder why there were no women in his life. Why there were never any women in his life.

He dumped a wad of bagged salad into a bowl and doused it with Greek dressing. When the steak was medium rare, he plated it and went to the kitchen table, with the salad. He cut off a big bite of steak and made a face when it turned out to be tough.

One of these days, his old friends were going to figure out why he kept dodging their attempts to fix him up. It was going to dawn on them that he was gay.

Wade dreaded that day. Even though he and Emily were the same age, she was his aunt by marriage. Her brother Russ was married to Wade's mother. If Jason and Emily knew, it wouldn't be long until his entire family, as well as everyone, knew.

It would absolutely kill him if his mother found out.

Wade dumped half the steak in the trash. He didn't want anyone to find out, especially his mother. There had already been way too much ugliness in her life, and she'd put up with a lot of shit for his sake, most of it on his behalf. No way was he inflicting any more pain on his mom. She'd put up with enough of the bad seeds making up the Baxter family. His mother didn't need to know that her ex's son, who she'd adopted when he was twelve, was as bad a seed as the rest of the Baxter clan.

He got out his iPad and was in the second level of Besiege when his phone dinged and a text message flashed across the screen.

Want to go for coffee? O. Aldrete

Wade sucked in his breath. *Owen had reached out to him.* With trembling fingers he grabbed the phone.

W: *Sure. When are you free?*
O: *Any time. Do you have rehearsal tomorrow?*
W: *Ends at nine. After that?*

O: *Sure. Hilda's Waffles on Heubner?*
W: *Works for me. See you about 9:15.*
Owen replied with a thumbs-up.

Wade smiled and breathed a sigh of relief. He'd figured right. Owen was interested, and by suggesting Hilda's, he understood Wade's desire to keep things private. Hilda's was dark and out of the way, and people mostly kept to themselves. They were in little danger of running into someone they knew. Their privacy was virtually guaranteed. Nobody was going to notice two men having coffee in a back booth. Wade's anonymity would be protected and nobody was going to see the scars that bothered Owen.

Owen got it.

Wade had been right.

Owen was going to be the perfect boyfriend.

***

Wade pulled into the empty parking place beside the front door of Hilda's. The lot was virtually empty but for two cars. Business tended to be slow in San Antonio coffee shops this time of day, between dinnertime for senior citizens and the late-night influx from the closing bars. He looked around. A couple of punk kids were wolfing down pancakes in a booth at the front, and a man sat by himself in the back who'd positioned himself so his face wasn't readily visible.

Wade's heart pounded in his throat as he approached the booth. "Owen?" he asked quietly. "Sorry I'm late."

Owen looked up. "'Sokay. Rehearsals never end when they tell you they will. Especially if Aubrey Ellis is directing."

They shook hands, Owen's fingers warm in his.

Wade slid into the booth across from Owen. "Aubrey's directed productions you were in?"

"Three or four. She directed the last production I did for them. Before..." He flicked his hand in front of his face.

They studied one another in the muted light of the coffee shop. Wade didn't know what to say. From his silence, Owen probably didn't either. This close, the scars on Owen's face were clearly visible, as were the ones on his left arm and hand. But they didn't detract from his appeal.

He wasn't wearing his usual hoodie or ball cap, and his black, wavy hair framed his face. An intricate tattoo peeked out from under the collar of his tee. Wade had to fight the urge to lean across the booth and take Owen's face between his hands and pull him closer for a kiss. Only the knowledge they were in public kept his hands firmly by his side. That, and not knowing if Owen was as turned-on as Wade was. The man's gaze was inscrutable as he stared across the booth.

A tired-looking waitress came to the booth. "What can I getcha?"

Wade's stomach growled. "Big breakfast number three. Iced tea instead of coffee."

She turned to Owen. "The eggs and sausage combo. Coffee."

The waitress ambled toward the kitchen. They continued to study one another.

"Are you out?" Wade blurted. "Wait, no, I mean—"

Owen reached out and laid his hand on Wade's arm. "It's a fair question. And, yeah, I'm out. I didn't stand on the rooftop and shout about it like some of my friends have, but I make no secret of my sexual orientation."

"What made you decide to come out?"

Owen's face hardened a little. "Life's too damned short to spend it living a lie." Again he gestured to his face. "I almost died getting these. Nearly kicking the bucket made me think. I'm gay. I have no reason to hide it or lie about it. Somebody doesn't like it, that's their problem, not mine."

Wade's lips twitched. "Tell me what you really think."

Owen smiled, ruefully. "How about you?"

"I haven't come out. And don't intend to."

Owen looked disapproving. "Why not? Why haven't you told your friends?"

"Because the one time I did, I got the shit knocked out of me. I haven't told anyone else."

He started to say more, to admit that he had a lot of ugliness inside him. But he stopped himself. He hardly knew this man. And airing dirty laundry on a first date was a sure-fire way not to get a second one.

"Maybe you told the wrong friend."

"Ya think?" He gestured around the diner. "My turn to ask a question. If you're out of the closet and you don't care if people know you're gay, why did you want to meet here?"

"Would you believe the great food?" Owen deadpanned.

"It's good, but not that good."

Owen gestured to his face again. "I hate to be seen in public. I hate the stares, the whispers and the gasps. It gets old."

Wade cocked his head and stared at Owen. "I've seen worse."

"So have I. But I still don't like showing them to the world."

"How'd it happen?"

"Trying to defuse a bomb."

The waitress dropped off their drinks, and Owen stirred his hot coffee.

"My damn fool partner took a chance he shouldn't have and the bomb went off. Killed Robby and damned near killed me."

The waitress put their plates in front of them. Wade looked at his plate and then Owen's much smaller one.

"That's not much food," he noted. "Did you eat earlier?"

"No. I pushed a mouse all day. And I'm not twenty-three anymore. If I don't watch it at least some, I balloon."

Wade eyed what he could see of Owen across the table. "Whatever you're eating or not eating, you look great."

Owen gave him a *yeah, right* look.

"I mean it," he insisted, even as his face reddened. "You look good."

Owen smiled, faintly. "Thanks. So do you."

They dug into their meals and the table was quiet for a few minutes.

Wade finally laid his fork on his empty plate. "That hit the spot."

"And he ate the whole thing," Owen teased.

He held Wade's gaze, and Wade felt himself blush again.

"What do you do to burn it all off? Besides being young."

"DOT engineer by day, in and out of a pickup, and crawling up on half-built bridges. J. Pierrepont Finch at night. At least until Christmas. I average three shows a year with the Durango. The dancing burns it off."

"Letti and I used to do two or three. I think she's doing most of them these days."

Wade thought back. "She crewed the last one we did at the old theater, and she acted in *Little Shop*. She's playing Hedy LaRue in *How to Succeed*."

Owen leaned back and sipped his coffee. "God, I miss it. I miss it more than I do being a cop."

"What do you do now?"

"Webpage design. Police departments, mostly. Steady work. Not as lucrative as being on the police force, but I have my disability retirement and can take care of my kids."

Wade cocked his head and studied Owen. "Your scars aren't that bad. Honestly. You could go back on stage if you wanted to."

"I don't think so. I'd have to audition and land a role. There are too many good-looking guys out there. They aren't gonna cast me." The side of his mouth curled up. "It's okay."

It wasn't okay and they both knew it.

Wade started to argue but thought better of it. Owen might be right. On the other hand, he'd be surprised if Josh and Rachel passed on his kind of talent because of a little scarring.

The waitress brought them the check. They raced to get out their wallets, and Owen beat Wade by a hair.

"You can pay next time."

A thrill ran down Wade's back. There was going to be a next time.

Loath to leave, Wade asked for a refill on his drink, and Owen did the same.

"Okay. I'll go first." Owen gave Wade a small smile. "I'm from Benecia, California. It's a small town in the Bay area. I met Letti in acting school. I knocked her up." Wade's brows went up, and Owen said, "Young, dumb, and full of come." Wade shook his head and laughed. "We moved to Texas 'cause Letti's father got me into the police academy."

"Ah." Wade nodded. That explained a lot. "I grew up in the Hill Country, in a lake community. My father married my mother when she was barely nineteen, and saddled her with his kid. She has a heart of gold and adopted me when I was twelve."

"Lucky kid."

"Yeah. She's special. Helped keep me right, and I went to Texas A and M. You ever hear about our traditions?"

"Some."

"My favorite was throwing your senior ring into a pitcher of beer and draining the whole thing to retrieve the ring, in your teeth. More than one has been swallowed over the years. I almost swallowed mine." He held out his left hand. "My proudest possession, except for maybe my cowboy boots."

"Gotta admit, you Aggies are something else." Owen laughed.

Wade looked at his phone and grimaced. "It's almost midnight. As great as this has been, I have to get up in the morning."

"Ahh, the beauty of being self-employed. I can sleep as late as I want," Owen teased.

"But I bet you've been known to work late into the night."

"You got that right."

They left the booth and walked out to the parking lot. Wade breathed in the night air, acutely aware of the man walking inches away from him. Oft-laundered jeans encased powerful thighs and a butt to die for, and muscles bulged under the tight tee shirt. A tattoo peeked out from under the collar.

This close, he could detect a faint whiff of sandalwood soap, aftershave, and an underlying essence that was pure Owen. Wade ached to wrap his arms around Owen and kiss the life out of him. He didn't know for sure, but every instinct told him Owen, too, felt the attraction.

A couple new cars had parked since Wade had gone inside.

"Which one's yours?" Owen asked.

"The pickup."

They walked together toward the truck.

"So how about next weekend? Are you in rehearsals?" Owen asked.

Wade's heart pounded in his chest. Owen was asking him for a date.

"Not in the evenings. What would you like to do?"

Owen thought a minute. "Do you like blow-em-ups? There's a new one coming out this weekend."

"Damn. I love blow-em-ups."

And a movie theater wasn't nearly as public as a busy restaurant.

"Then that's what we'll do." Owen reached out and drew Wade closer. "I can't wait another minute. I have to kiss you." He looked at Wade with a question in his eyes. "Or do you not..."

"Not normally. No. But damn. I have to kiss you too." Wade swayed toward Owen before he stiffened. "No, wait. Somebody might see us."

"So what if they do?"

"I-I…" Wade whirled around and hit the unlock button on his key fob. "Get in the truck."

He threw open the back door and scrambled inside. Owen leaped in after him and bore him down into the bench seat, pressing his lips firmly to Wade's.

There was nothing tentative or gentle in Owen's embrace. His lips were demanding as he took possession of Wade's mouth, leaving his brand on Wade's lips. Wade snaked his arms around Owen's neck, drawing the man even closer. They were plastered together from lips to knees.

Owen's chest was warm and hard against Wade's, his thighs thick and powerful, and his erection undeniable. Wade's fingers caressed Owen's nape before curling into his soft, wavy hair. Owen's hands were hard as they caressed Wade's shoulders and back.

Wade's erection swelled against Owen's powerful body. He'd lived. Had been in a few relationships, but this—this was like nothing he'd ever felt in any other man's arms. His body throbbed. He was on fire for this man.

They kissed and caressed each other for long moments, both holding on tight. Finally, Owen raised his head. In the dim light of the backseat, he looked dazed.

"Fuck, that was good," he breathed.

"Yeah." Wade stared into Owen's eyes. "You're a helluva kisser."

"Not bad yourself." Owen levered himself up and out of the pickup. "Saturday. I'll text you with a time. 'Night."

Wade sat up and watched Owen's fine ass as it and those long powerful thighs walked across the parking lot. Wade's heart pounded in his throat, and his erection strained painfully against his jeans. He didn't know what to think. Never in his life had he responded to a man the way he had Owen.

Wade could hardly wait to get him naked in a bed.

CHAPTER 4

Owen whistled under his breath as he took the exit ramp off I-10 close to the Medical Center. The sun was low in the sky on this late October evening, and the air was comfortably cool. Anticipation was sweet on his tongue as he followed his GPS under the expressway and down an artery until it turned into a subdivision of nice but hardly lavish homes.

He'd relived that incredible kiss too many times to count. And the feel of Wade's strong body beneath him, his lips soft and warm, his body hard and muscled, his thick cock poking Owen in the stomach were sensations he relived over and over. Especially when they'd inspired fantasies Owen took care of in the shower.

Damn. He hoped he got the chance to make some of those fantasies come true.

He snaked through the subdivision, finally ending up on a cul-de-sac, and spotted Wade's big-ass truck in a driveway. A sick-looking potted plant sat on the front porch, and while the house and yard were well-kept, they seemed somehow forlorn.

Owen rang the bell and Wade appeared a moment later, bare-chested with wet hair and a towel slung around his neck. Owen drank in the sight of strong pecs, liberally dusted with brown hair. A large maroon tattoo with the Texas A&M logo covered the left side of his chest.

"Sorry I'm not ready." He unlatched the screen to let Owen in. "I got off late from my mom's, in the Hill Country, and caught some bad construction traffic. On my own job, no less. Karma's not a nice lady."

"You go up to your mom's often?"

"Fairly often. Yesterday was my birthday. I got off early and drove up in the afternoon. They threw me a party last night. Mom loves to give a party."

"Well then, happy birthday."

Owen followed Wade into the house, his mouth practically watering at the sight of Wade's bare back, pale but rippling with muscle. A dark tan started about halfway down his upper arms and ringed his neck. Obviously, the young man was confident enough in his looks that he didn't worry about having a farmer's tan. Owen understood. He'd been the same way when he wore short-sleeved uniform shirts in the summer.

A long surgical scar with puckered pin scars on either side ran down Wade's left forearm. Owen wondered what had happened. Whatever it was, it was bound to have been painful.

Wade led him past a small living room, into a sparsely furnished family room that was pretty much empty.

"Can I get you anything to drink?" He peered into the refrigerator. "I've got beer or soda."

"Soda's fine."

Wade handed Owen a coke. "Have a seat. I'll be ready in a minute."

Owen popped open the soda can. His gaze was drawn to the bookcases flanking the big-screen TV and the myriad of framed pictures they held. Lots and lots of pictures of Wade with his theater friends, and, what Owen assumed, was his family.

Not one picture of Wade with a man.

Owen tamped down his irritation and reminded himself that his picture wall wasn't much different. But he did have a picture or two of the vacation he'd gone on with a lover a couple years back. He wondered where Wade kept the pictures he'd taken of his previous lovers. Or if he'd even taken any. Hopefully, he'd cared enough about the men to take at least a few pictures of them.

Wade returned in a couple minutes, dressed in a short-sleeved western shirt, boot-cut jeans, and the fanciest boots Owen had ever seen.

He whistled appreciatively. "You do clean up nice, country boy."

Wade made a production of looking him up and down. "So do you, city boy."

Owen had gone to great lengths to look nice this evening, wearing a black polo shirt, new black jeans and city-style boots, and a black fedora with a wide brim. There wasn't much he could do about his face, but he still had a body worth showing off.

"What time does the show start?" Wade asked.

Owen looked at his watch. "We better get moving."

The two of them climbed into Owen's car. Owen snickered when Wade had to push the seat back.

"Sorry. Sophie was there last. I took her to the museum this afternoon, to see the exhibit of Broadway stage costumes. Damn, some of those women were skinny."

"One of the virtues of the Durango. Josh never discriminates against plus-sized talent."

Owen glanced over at Wade. "Bet he pairs you with the big girls to do the lifts."

"Been known to happen. Was the visit worth it? Do I need to go?"

"You might find it interesting."

The parking lot was crowded. Owen pointed to the entrance and got out the tickets he'd printed online.

"Smooth," Wade said. "That's still new to me. I grew up going to a small-town single screen that showed first-run movies in thirty-five millimeter. Still does. One of the last ones left."

"Does it do any business?"

"You bet. It's either there or drive all the way to Austin. Everybody in town goes."

"It sounds storybook, growing up in the Hill Country, close to the lake."

Wade's face darkened. "Not always."

Owen looked at him in surprise. But the dark was gone and Wade was smiling again.

They stopped off at the concession stand for popcorn and sodas. Their seats were in the next to last row. Despite the crowded parking lot, this theater was only about three-quarters full, and most of the seats around them were empty. They were treated to the usual ridiculous number of trailers, and finally the movie began.

Owen could tell five minutes in, that, as per usual, the writers hadn't done their homework on police procedure. He groaned when a policeman started grilling a suspect.

"Jesus," he whispered. "No Miranda? They've got to be kidding."

"And he's cuffed in the front," Wade murmured. "A real cop would never do that. Unless he was mighty dumb."

"You know police stuff?"

"Probably not what you do, but Mom's husband was military police and then a deputy sheriff before he quit to run the vineyard. I learned a bit from being around him."

"Tell you what. Let's make it a contest. Hold my hand. Squeeze it when you spot an error. I'll do the same. Whoever spots the most procedural errors gets treated to a drink after the movie."

And a great excuse to hold Wade's hand.

"You're on."

Owen held out his hand. Wade slipped his hand into Owen's, palms rough and the tips of his fingers callused. Owen wondered how Wade's hands had gotten so rugged. Ranch work? Part of his job? It sure wasn't on the stage at the Durango. Wade's hand was considerably bigger than Owen's, his fingers longer and his palm wider. And it felt so right.

Wade spotted fourteen procedural errors. Owen, twenty-one.

"They really should've hired a consultant," Wade commented as they left the theater.

"But the story wouldn't have flowed anywhere near as smoothly. Sometimes it's up to the audience to indulge in the suspension of disbelief and go with the story."

"Like they do at the theater," Wade mused.

"Exactly."

"So where do you want to get the drink I owe you?'

Owen thought a minute. "There's a nice place down on North Main. Quiet, private. I've been there a few times."

"Do any of the theater people go there?" Wade asked.

Owen fought back irritation. "Never seen anybody from the theater. They tend to hang out at that pizza place or the bar down from the theater. Nobody's gonna see us, if that's what's worrying you."

Wade's face cleared. "Then let's go."

They were halfway to the bar and engaged in a lively discussion of the upcoming election when Owen's phone rang. "Five will get you ten it's a telemarketer," Wade stated as Owen fished out his phone.

"Screen says SAPD. What the—?" He clicked on his phone.

"Mr. Aldrete? This is the San Antonio Police Department. Your ex-wife gave me this number. She and your daughter were involved in an accident this evening. They're both en route to the Medical Center."

"*What?* Letti and Sophie in a wreck? What happened? Are they all right?"

"Another car ran a red light and broadsided Ms. Aldrete's car. As far as their condition, the EMT's determined that they both needed medical treatment. That's all I know."

Owen tossed his phone to Wade and did a U-turn in the middle of the street. "Letti and Sophie were in a wreck. I've got to get to the hospital."

"Are they all right?" Wade asked.

"Why would they be on their way to the hospital if they were all right?" he snapped. "Jesus, I'm sorry. I didn't mean that like it came out. It's... that girl is my life, and Letti and I... hell."

"I get it," Wade said. "She's the mother of your children. You still have feelings for her. You'd have to."

"Thanks for understanding. God, what I wouldn't give for lights and a siren about now."

They sped down the street and Owen pulled onto the expressway. "We'll be there in a minute."

Owen hit the gas and flew down the highway. Wade sat silently until they flew by the exit to his house.

"You passed the exit."

"No, I didn't. The emergency room exit's one up." He turned disbelieving eyes on Wade. "Surely you didn't expect me to take the time to drop you off."

"It would've taken you five minutes at the most." Wade's voice was tight.

"Five minutes is a long damned time when my daughter's life might be at stake."

"Whatever."

Jesus. What an ass.

Owen pulled into the first available space in the emergency room parking lot. He ran to the door, not caring whether Wade followed him, and screeched to a halt in front of the intake window.

"Sophie and Letti Aldrete. Where are they?"

The nurse turned to him with a bored expression. "They were admitted a few minutes ago." She gestured to the waiting room. "Someone will come get you when you can go back."

"What the hell do you mean? That's my daughter and her mother in there. I need to go to them. *Now.*"

She flicked her eyes up and down. "You a doctor?"

"*What?*"

"Are you a doctor? A nurse? A health care professional who's going to do them some good?"

Owen shook his head.

"Then sit down over there and let the professionals do their job. They'll call you back when they've finished."

Owen felt a hand on his shoulder. "Chill, Owen. She's right. You can't do them any good, and you'll be in the way."

Owen looked up. Wade had come in, after all.

He let Wade lead him to a chair. Wade pushed him down and sat beside him with his hands clasped in front of him.

"You want platitudes?"

"Nah. I want for my daughter and her mother to be all right."

"Fair enough."

They sat in silence. Unlike in the movie theater, Wade was careful not to touch him. Not that he wanted him to, Owen told himself. Wade might have come in, but he'd been an ass in the car, expecting Owen to drop him off so they wouldn't be seen together. Wade was probably sweating blood right now, hoping to hell none of the theater people came to the hospital and found out his dirty little secret.

What a chickenshit.

It felt like hours, but only thirty minutes passed before a nurse stuck his head out the door.

"Aldrete? You can come on back."

Owen jumped out of the chair. "How are they?"

"Sprains. Superficial cuts. Nasty bruises. Nothing serious."

"Thank God." He was hot on the nurse's heels as the man led him through the maze of cubicles, finally stopping at two with the middle curtain open. Letti was on one stretcher, and Sophie the other. Letti had on a neck collar, and Sophie's right arm was in a sling, and they both had small cuts on their faces. They were both conscious, and turned identical bleary eyes on him. Owen felt tears rush to his eyes. The nurse was right. They were better, way better than he'd expected them to be.

"How 'ya doin'?"

"I hurt, Daddy. My arm's sore. At least the play was last week. I couldn't have done it like this."

He felt a small smile touch his lips. "Ever the trouper." He leaned over and placed a gentle kiss on Sophie's cheek, and then turned to Letti. "How are you feeling?"

"Like an elephant sat on my chest. I have seatbelt bruises from hell, and my neck hurts like a son of a bitch. Thank God the production's over and I don't have to get up on that stage feeling like this. On the other hand, maybe this is how Audrey felt."

"At least your sense of humor's intact."

"I wish the damned car was. Sucker's totaled."

"Cars can be replaced. You and Sophie can't."

He started to offer to help her find a new one but stopped himself. She'd been fiercely independent since the divorce and wouldn't want his input.

"Can I take the two of you home?"

"They want us to stay overnight, for observation. What you could do, if you would, is get out my insurance card and go do the mountain of paperwork they're gonna want. My wallet's in the bag under the stretcher."

He fished out her wallet and made his way back through the maze to the admitting desk. He looked over at where he and Wade had been sitting. The chair was empty. The motherfucker had booked as soon as they found out Letti and Sophie were all right.

Asshole.

Owen fumed as he filled out form after form. The little pissant had run out on him. On him and a woman and girl who'd acted with him on numerous occasions, that he supposedly cared about. He was more concerned about keeping his secret than he was about them.

To hell with Wade Baxter. Owen didn't need that kind of shit for a boyfriend. He'd find someone else. Someone who wasn't ashamed of being who he was.

When he finished wading through the last of the paperwork, he trudged back to Sophie and Letti, who were now in hospital gowns.

"They're cleaning a room for us now," Sophie informed him.

Owen pointed to the gowns. "Love the sleepwear. Alluring."

Sophie snickered.

Letti shook her head. "Your sense of humor's still intact, too." She looked him up and down. "You're sure dressed nice for your usual Saturday night appointment with Netflix."

He shrugged. "I was on a date when the department called."

Sophie's face broke into a smile. "You were? Good for you, Daddy. You need to get out of that apartment sometimes."

Letti sat up straighter. "You had a date? Anybody I know?"

Boy, do you. "Nobody important."

"If he was nobody important, then why are you dressed to the nines?" she pressed.

Owen shrugged. "Gotta look nice sometimes. Look, he's a chickenshit nobody I won't be seeing again. Lay off with the inquisition and tell me what time you want me here in the morning."

***

Wade dumped the sack of candy into the plastic jack-o-lantern and gathered up the neatly lettered sign and walked them out to the front porch. The sun hadn't set yet, but the streets and sidewalks were filling with eager trick-or-treaters dressed in every costume imaginable, looking to score candy and trinkets.

Wade let the wistfulness roll over him as he placed the jack-o-lantern and the sign reading, "One only or I shall haunt you" on the step. It was times like this, seeing the other gaily costumed children, that he missed Noelle the most. The delightful child had loved Halloween with a passion, the candy and the costumes, and pretending to be an elf or a fairy. Or a munchkin. Wade sighed. He missed her mother, too. Even though there was nothing romantic between him and Sandra, she and Noelle had filled an important niche in his life. One that would most likely never be filled again.

He went back in the house and slipped into a pair of tennis shoes and an old A&M tee. Maybe the melancholy had nothing to do with Sandra and Noelle. He hadn't been able to get his head out of his ass since Saturday night, when he texted an Uber to pick him up at the hospital. His first reaction on seeing the car was immense relief. He'd gotten away in time, before the expected influx of concerned theater people and Letti's mom and grandmother.

Guilt hit him about halfway home. He'd only waited long enough to get a preliminary report from the doctor. He hadn't waited to talk to Owen. He hadn't waited to see them for himself. He hadn't offered to help. He'd left Owen holding the bag, and gotten out of there as quickly as he could.

Shame had tormented him ever since.

He didn't have to run away. He could have stayed, supported his friends, done something constructive. Instead, he'd let his fear rule, and booked. He'd been so frightened of revealing who he really was, he'd been a coward and an ass. He could only imagine what Owen thought of him.

But if he'd stayed, he would have outted himself to the theater community. And if they knew, it wouldn't be long before the rest of the world did, too. There was no way he could risk that.

Instead, he'd nipped a promising relationship in the bud. He'd not heard back from Owen, not even to tell him that Sophie and Letti were okay. He'd had to hear that from Rachel, Monday night at rehearsal. Not that he expected to hear from Owen. The man was out and accepted himself completely. He expected other gay men to do the same. And from what Owen had implied, he had contempt for those who couldn't or wouldn't accept themselves.

Owen didn't understand where Wade was coming from, and never would.

At least he'd respected Wade's desire for privacy. He must not have said a word to Letti, because if he had, gossip would be buzzing around the theater like flies around a dead bird. The open-minded Durango crowd wouldn't have cared he was gay, but they most certainly would have talked about it.

Wade checked the porch light and locked the front door. Mindful of all the families on the streets, he drove through the neighborhood more carefully than usual, and breathed a sigh of relief when he reached the expressway. If only Owen could understand. But he didn't and he wouldn't, and Wade couldn't fight it. From Owen's point of view, he was right and Wade was the one in the wrong. Maybe Owen *was* right. But Wade had his reasons for feeling the way he did about coming out. And those reasons weren't going away any time soon.

He pulled onto the expressway and hit the gas. That kiss had rocked Wade's world. He'd relived it in his mind many times, his cock growing hard at the mere thought of Owen's hands on his body as their lips fused together.

Owen had a lot more going for him than sex appeal. He was funny and personable and sharp as a tack. And brimming with so much talent. Talent that was being wasted for no real reason. With some of Wade's mother's makeup, there were plenty of parts Owen could play. Wade wished there was some way to get Owen involved at the theater. Even if a relationship with the man wasn't in the cards, they needed Owen at the Durango.

Wade slowed down again as he exited the expressway. The streets around the theater thronged with costumed revelers, mostly children, but a few adults were in costumes. He took the last parking place on the street.

The front doors to the Academy were open and the cast members playing the main characters of *How to Succeed* were milling around in the lobby chatting with parents waiting for their children to finish their evening classes. Through the half-open doors he could see their Academy director teaching a dance class to the older kids.

"Since when does Jessica have to teach the classes herself?" he asked Josh, who was standing in the doorway.

"Since she's had three instructors quit on her in the last three weeks. Two of them followed their boyfriends to wherever, and the third took a new day job in Dallas. I hope they don't live to regret it. In the meantime, Jessica's looking for new teachers, and she and Rachel are covering the gaps."

"If she needs help, I'm a phone call away."

"Thanks. I'll make sure I remind her of that."

The class finished a few minutes later. The dancers drifted through the lobby, two or three at a time, followed by a giggling group of tweens who'd been in a singing class, and then a bunch of the youngest age group who'd been with Miss Shirley in an acting class.

The parents and the kids wandered out, leaving the actors. Director Aubrey Ellis divided them into the specific scenes they were rehearsing, and assigned them to different rehearsal rooms.

Wade and Danica Sauceda, the young drama teacher cast as Rosemary Pilkington, were sent to the rehearsal room in the back, with instructions to practice the dialogue and singing, "It's Been a Long Day." Danica wasn't the actress Sandra was, but she was a pleasure to work with, and they soon had the scene down to Aubrey's exacting standards.

Danica was sent to rehearse elsewhere, and Josh took Danica's place.

"So, you're the book," Wade teased as Josh held the manuscript in front of him. "Must be nice not having to memorize a script."

"Ya think?"

Josh turned over the manuscript and laid it facedown on the chair. His eyes dancing, he then quoted every word of the book's first soliloquy.

"Well, never mind," Wade said. "Why'd you memorize it?"

"I'm lucky. Three or four run-throughs and I have pretty much anything memorized."

"You lucky bastard. I have to work at it."

Josh winked. "It must not be that hard for you, given the lines you've memorized for us." He picked up the manuscript. "I wish I didn't have to do this one, though."

"Why?"

"Wrong kind of voice. I sound young. Which is great for a lot of roles. Not the book." He sat beside Wade. "I'd give anything if Owen Aldrete would come in and do this one for us. Letti said they played J. Pierrepont and Rosemary years ago, in a production up in Boerne, which would give him a feel for the part."

"I thought he was a baritone. The part's written for a tenor."

"Letti said he's got an unbelievable range."

"Has anyone approached him about it?"

"Nah. What good would it do? The only reason he came in and did Audrey II for us that night was because he felt like he owed Cameron, and was able to stay off-stage. Owen doesn't care about the theater anymore, and I don't feel like wasting my breath."

Wade bit his lip. Owen most certainly did care about the theater. The man missed it like a son of a bitch. But if Wade pointed that out, Josh would want to know how Wade knew that.

Voicing the book would be the perfect way for Owen to ease back into acting. Wade was going to tell him so. A relationship wasn't going to happen, but Wade would be damned if he didn't at least try to get Owen involved again at the Durango.

He and Josh went through some of the scenes where J. Pierrepont Finch was reading from the book. Aubrey called a halt to rehearsals at ten and sent them all out the door, reminding them they had rehearsals later in the week. Wade was unlocking his truck, when Letti came out the door and clicked open a new car parked near his.

"I like the new wheels," he said as she walked toward the car.

"Not looking forward to the payment. But you do what you gotta do."

He walked up to her and gave her a gentle hug. Up close, he could see a few healing cuts on her forehead and cheeks. Nothing serious, and thankfully, nothing that would scar her gorgeous face.

"Rachel called me about the wreck. How are you feeling?"

"A little sore. A lot broke. Between the car and the hospital co-pay. Sheesh. At least Owen picked up Sophie's co-pay."

"I'm sure he did. He's her father."

Letti shrugged. "He has his uses." Her eyes danced. "You should have seen him Saturday night. Dolled up like I haven't seen him in years. New duds. Fancy hat. The works. We interrupted his evening big-time." She laughed out loud. "The asshole was actually out on a date."

Wade's heart jumped in his chest. Had Owen said something, after all?

"He was out on a date?"

"Must not have been much of one. I asked him who he was with, and he made some crack about the guy being a 'chickenshit nobody.' Guess the evening wasn't going well." She looked at her watch. "Gotta run. That alarm rings earlier and earlier these days."

Wade wished her a good evening through stiff lips. His face flamed and he was grateful for the cover of darkness.

"A chickenshit nobody."

That certainly left him in no doubt how Owen felt about him. Even though he'd already known how Owen probably felt, hearing it from Letti's lips still stung.

But then, Wade wasn't the only one who was a chickenshit. Josh was right. Owen's voice was perfect to play the part of the book. He wouldn't be seen by the audience, but he was so scared that somebody might stare at his less than perfect face that he hid all the time, either at home or behind a hat or hoodie, and let his talent go to waste.

The crowds had thinned and Wade made good time getting home. He dumped the empty jack-o-lantern and the sign, on the sofa and sat at his computer. It didn't take him long to bring up a list of people-finding websites. He entered Owen's name, and it didn't take but a few minutes before he had an address, with an apartment number.

Mapping it placed the apartment a couple miles from Letti's house. He looked at his phone. It was too late to go by Owen's tonight. Wade had to get up in the morning. But tomorrow evening, after his grandparents' charity gala, he was going to arm himself with a pepperoni pizza and a boatload of chutzpah.

He was going to get Owen back to the Durango.

CHAPTER 5

Owen stared at the large-screen television mounted on the wall as the latest episode of *Homicide Hunters* ended with the inevitable arrest of the perpetrator. He'd gotten hooked on the stories during his long and painful recovery from the explosion, and eagerly waited for the latest installment of the old detective's cases.

Owen loved true crime shows. He loved matching his wits against the professionals who solved the crimes, and a good bit of the time he had the answer before they did. Sometimes he wished he'd gone into vice or homicide instead of the bomb squad. If he had, maybe he wouldn't have gotten his ass blown up. But at the time, it had been the fastest route of advancement and he'd had kids to feed and a house payment to make. No point in playing what-if or second-guessing himself at this late date. What was done was done.

He muted the television and looked around the living room. This damn place was lonely. It was homey enough, but too quiet. He missed the noise his kids made, their music and their chatter, and their raised voices when Marco invaded Sophie's domain.

Owen missed the sound of Letti singing the songs from whatever show she was doing while she cooked dinner. He missed having to holler, "Turn it down" when one of them cranked up the latest pop song to ear-splitting volume. He thought back to Wade's empty, forlorn-looking family room and wondered if Wade got as lonely as Owen did.

His lips firmed. If Wade was lonely, it was his own damned fault. Owen didn't have much of a choice, given his ruined face. But Wade was young and heartbreakingly handsome, and could have any guy he wanted. Holing up in that house and lying to the world about himself was his choice. He didn't have to do that.

Anger still burned when Owen remembered that empty chair in the waiting room. Wade could have at least waited for Owen to come back out. Instead, he'd run off like the chickenshit that he was.

Owen would rather be lonely than put up with a coward like Wade.

He flipped through the shows he'd recorded and was deep into the restoration of a '63 Chevy when someone knocked on the door. Owen paused the show and glanced at his watch. It was almost ten. The only person who ever came to see him this late was Sophie. His face wreathed in a smile, he threw open the front door. "Sophie, princess, how—" His words froze on his lips.

Wade stood in the doorway dressed in a tuxedo and holding an oversized, delicious smelling pizza box and a six-pack of Corona. He wasn't smiling and had a determined expression on his face. "What are you doing here? Surely you don't think I want to go out with you again," Owen ground out.

"I'm sure you don't. That's not why I came over tonight. I need to talk to you. I came bearing food and beer to bribe you into letting me in." Damn. Owen's stomach growled. The nuked hot dog he ate for supper hadn't gone far.

"I don't want to talk to you." His stomach growled even louder.

Wade looked at it and laughed. "But you would love this pizza, wouldn't you? The price of this mushroom and pepperoni delight, and the adult libations that go with it, is that you have to listen to me for a few minutes. Then I'll be out of your hair."

"Why would I want to listen to a chickenshit like you?"

Wade's face hardened. "Because you're as big a damned chickenshit as I am. Now, do you let me in, or do I leave your stomach growling and take this home and eat it by myself?"

Chickenshit. *Him?* The pissant had to be kidding.

Owen's back went up. "Fine. Come in. I'd love to hear where in the world you get off calling me a chickenshit."

"Be happy to oblige." Wade skirted around Owen and headed for the kitchen. "Where're your plates?"

Owen elbowed Wade aside and set the small dining room table. Wade opened two beers and put the pizza box between them. He opened the box and the incredible aroma filled the room.

Wade took a huge slice and pointed to the box. "Chow down."

"Whatever." Owen snagged an equally big slice of the oversized pizza. Despite his anger, he managed to kill his half of the huge pie. He drained the first Corona and opened another and drank down nearly half the second.

Then he leaned back and crossed his arms in front of him. "What's with the tuxedo? You decide I was worth dressing up for?"

Wade made a production of looking Owen up and down, taking in his ratty gym shorts, his faded muscle shirt, and the eye-patch covering his empty eye socket.

"Hardly. You rock the pirate look, however." Owen chuckled. "Gramps and Gran had their presentation gala tonight. They awarded their grant to the Durango."

"And you still ate half a pizza? Do you ever do anything besides eat?"

"Once in a while."

"So, now that you've softened me up, tell me why I'm as big a chickenshit as you. I'm not the one hiding who he is from the world."

Wade leaned back and mirrored Owen's pose. "No, you're hiding out in this apartment, letting life go by because your face is a less than perfect. You're wasting your talent because somebody might look at you twice."

Owen breathed out in a rush. "Maybe I do. Maybe I got sick of the horrified stares when I go out in public. Didn't you notice the way people looked at me at the movie theater the other night?"

"You mean, that hot chick in the short shorts undressing you with her eyes? Yeah, I noticed."

Owen snorted. "She wasn't undressing me. She was undressing you."

Wade smiled, wickedly. "Nope. That was you, asshole. She said something to her friend about not knowing Fedoras could be so sexy." He leaned forward. "The scars are not that bad, Owen. Honestly."

"Yeah, they are."

"Let me show you something." Wade got out his phone and scrolled a few minutes. He handed the phone to Owen. "Take a good look at Jason. That's what I call bad. His face is bad. Not yours."

Owen stared down at the picture and couldn't control the wince. It was an informal family portrait of a man and woman with two little boys. The redheaded woman was sweet-looking, and the boys must've favored their father, but he couldn't tell because the guy's features were mostly gone. The poor bastard's face was nothing but a mass of scar tissue. No hair, no ears, not much in the way of a nose or lips left. His arms and hands were also badly scarred, and Owen could only imagine what he looked like under his clothes.

"My college roommate," Wade muttered. "Jason Donahue. Iraq, twenty-o-four. Blown up by a suicide bomber. Burned over half his body. Seriously reduced lung capacity. Can't control his body temperature, and has to stay covered in the sun. Years of surgeries. He lost most of his twenties to the burns, and didn't get his degree until he was thirty years old."

Owen looked down at the picture again. "She must have really loved him. To stick beside him through all that."

"Nope. Not the way it happened. She met him years later. Emily never saw him before he was burned. Scars and all, he managed to catch a lovely woman. Ten years younger than him, and an heiress, no less. Not that they really need her trust fund. Jason makes a shit-pile of money on his own."

"Doing what?"

"Selling cars."

"*Selling cars?*"

"Actually, he's moved way up in management. But, yeah. He worked a showroom looking like that. And he still meets the public every damned day. So forgive me if I'm not too impressed with you hiding out here so the world won't see your little boo-boos."

"Fine. We've established that I'm a chickenshit. But what about you? You may get out on that stage, but you're living a lie. You're not honest about who you are. If anyone is gonna be okay with who you really are, it's your friends at the Durango."

Wade dropped his eyes. "If it was only them, it might be all right. But I'm an engineer at the Texas Department of Transportation. We're not in California, man. My colleagues wouldn't *feel* me."

"Do the folks at your office sit around discussing their sex lives?"

"No. At least, not in front of me."

"They don't discuss theirs, and you don't discuss yours. I don't see the problem. I'm not suggesting you put it all over social media or take out an ad in the paper. I'm saying there's no reason to hide it so deeply, at least not at the Durango."

"My family attends every one of my productions. If the folks at the Durango know, somebody might slip and say something in front of Mom. She's the last one I want to find out about me."

Owen raised his eyebrow. "Your mom's a homophobe?"

"It's not something I want her to have to cope with."

"If you say so. But it's totally ridiculous to hide who you are from your friends at the Durango."

"It's totally ridiculous for you to hide out here and not get involved at the theater again."

They stared at one another for a moment.

"Why did you come over tonight?" Owen asked. "What was the purpose of this visit?"

Wade's stare bore into him. "They need someone to voice the book in *How to Succeed*. Josh and I rehearsed tonight. He doesn't sound right, and he's fretting about it. He sounds like a little kid delivering. They need you for the role. They need you to voice the book." He leaned forward. "It would be perfect. The book is voiced from off-stage. You'd never be seen by the audience. You could have it both ways. You'd put that incredible talent to work again and still have your anonymity." He leaned back. "They need you. And you need them."

Owen's heart pounded in his throat. Longing filled him as he thought of being back in the theater. Wearing a mic. Delivering the perfect line. Singing his heart out. Dancing his way across the stage. Not that he would get to do all of that, or even much of that, as the book. But he would be back at the theater. He would be doing something he loved, but he'd being going out on a limb.

He looked at Wade and narrowed his eyes. He wasn't the only one who needed to go out on a limb. Wade needed to break out of his shell and be honest about who he was. Okay, maybe not with the whole world, but at least with his friends at the Durango. They would think nothing of it. They would love him just the same.

"I'll do it on one condition," he said when Wade's face lit up. "If you'll meet me for a beer and some buffalo wings Saturday night, at the bar and grille where the Durango crowd hangs out. I'll call Josh and see if it's too late to audition for the book."

Wade's face fell. "I told you I couldn't do that."

"That's my condition. Take it or leave it. You want me out on a limb, fine. But you gotta go out on one yourself."

"I'll have to think about it," he said slowly.

"Let me know what you decide. Thanks for the pizza."

Wade let himself out. Owen threw away the pizza box and put the dishes in the dishwasher. He doubted Wade would take him up on his deal.

Owen settled down on the sofa and hit "Play." The '63 Chevy was restored and the mechanics had moved on to a 1972 Gran Torino when his phone buzzed.

See you Saturday night. I'll tell Josh to expect your call.

Owen smiled and texted a thumbs-up.

***

Wade's mom's text had been a pleasant surprise. She and Russ were bringing his younger siblings to town for a break from life in the country, and she wanted to make sure it was all right to descend on him for the night. It didn't leave him much time to get things ready, but his family didn't expect perfection, and he always enjoyed their visits, especially the inevitable trip to the Mexican food dive his little brother loved.

Wade hauled the cot out of the closet and checked the time on his phone. His mom had texted a few minutes ago that they were about an hour out, which left him plenty of time for a shower. He strode naked through the house and stopped at the bathroom mirror and took a critical look at his body, pinching the flesh at his waist. Okay, but he'd picked up a few pounds from the fast food he'd eaten too often since Sandra's departure.

What would Owen think of his body? Wade hadn't had more than a couple one-night stands since Darius, his last lover, had walked out on him a year ago. Darius had been into him, but, like Owen, Darius couldn't understand why Wade was so determined to keep his homosexuality a secret. Darius hadn't been able to get him to change his mind, and had finally left him in disgust.

But Owen had. He'd gotten Wade to agree to go with him tomorrow night, to where the Durango crowd hung out. There was an almost one-hundred-percent chance there would be someone from the Durango in the bar.

He would be officially coming out of the closet to his friends at the Durango.

With Owen by his side, no less.

He looked down and laughed. His cock was already at half-mast. The mere thought of Owen Aldrete made him hard.

Wade wondered if his public outing would be their last date, or if they would continue to see one another afterward.

Ignoring his nervousness, he stepped into the shower, soaped down and washed the dust out of his hair. He looked down and sighed. Damn. His cock was like steel. Either he did something about it now or he put up with a hard-on all evening. He doused his hand with shampoo and imagined his hands were Owen's lips as he pumped his cock, hard and fast, gasping when he erupted, dousing the shower walls with his come. He rinsed himself off and pushed away all thoughts of Owen, otherwise, he'd be back in here all damn day.

He shaved and dressed and was loading the washer when the doorbell rang. Two hours later they were back in his place after having ploughed through copious amounts of Mexican food.

"So when do we get to see you up on the stage again?" Russ, Wade's stepfather, asked before he chugged down his beer.

"*How to Succeed* opens the Friday after Thanksgiving. But that's Black Friday, and you both like to be in the store that weekend. I could get you tickets for the first weekend in December. Does that work for you?"

His mom and Russ checked their phone calendars and nodded. Mom requested he tell them a little about the upcoming production.

"Danica's settling into the Rosemary Pilkington part. She's doing okay."

"But she's not Sandra, is she?" his mother asked softly.

"No, she isn't. Sandra would have knocked it out of the park."

"I know you miss her," his mother said. "You miss them both."

"I do. But it's hard to be mad at her for going back to her husband. She and Noelle are happy. That's all that matters."

"I was surprised the little pissant came around," Russ said thoughtfully. "He didn't impress me much."

"He got better," Wade said.

"He needed to," Russ stated dryly.

Wade waited tensely for his mother to make the expected, *You need to find a nice girl,* comment, but she said nothing of the kind, instead changing the subject.

They talked for a few minutes about other things, before Russ took Mom by the hand and led her to the guest bedroom. Wade popped open another beer and went out on the patio to drink it. The air was cool and crisp this late, and a few stars were visible, shining through the city lights.

His mother and the man she'd married were wonderful. He thought about his plans tomorrow night, and his stomach clenched. He couldn't imagine what his mother and Russ would think if they found out he was gay.

Russ would be horrified. He'd served in the Army for years and ate nails for breakfast. The man was as macho as they came. And his mother. God, how could he do that to her? She'd already put up with so much from his father and from his grandmother for his sake. If his homosexuality became public knowledge, she'd have to put up with so much more. He could only imagine the abuse his homophobic uncles would heap upon her head for raising a Baxter to be a queer. And her conservative neighbors in Verde and Heaven's Point would scorn her at best, and, most likely, deride her. He owed it to her to protect her from the fallout. She'd been damn good to him over the years. She finally had a happy life. She deserved to keep it.

But he couldn't back out on Owen. Josh had done a happy dance last night at rehearsal.

"Owen's gonna do the book. I don't know what made him, but he called and offered to do the voice for us. Hot damn. Aldrete's back."

Wade would be damned if he gave Owen an excuse to back out.

Tomorrow night: the bar and grille for beer and Buffalo wings, and honesty with his friends at the Durango. He'd come out to them. And he hoped to hell they kept the news to themselves when his family came around.

CHAPTER 6

Wade parked his truck in the Durango lot and hoofed it down the street. The parking lot and street around the Thirties Bar and Grille was jammed with vehicles. The bar, new but designed to blend into the deco neighborhood, was popular with the locals, and had become a favorite watering hole for the Durango crowd since they moved into the new theater. He stepped in and took a deep breath as he scanned the room. No familiar faces. But there would be before the night was through. Somebody from the Durango was bound to show up.

The hostess seated him at the requested back booth. He ordered a beer and a plate of Buffalo wings. His waitress was heading to him with his beer when Owen walked in the door without his signature hat or hoodie. He looked around and his lips firmed until he spotted Wade at the far end of the room. His face cleared and he sauntered over and slid in beside Wade. "Hiding back here?" he gibed.

Wade shook his head. "You go stand in the middle of the room with the TV blaring and everybody trying to talk over it and see if that's where you want to sit. I prefer to sit where I can actually have a conversation."

"Good point."

"Besides, we're perfectly visible here. You found me. If it makes you feel better, wave at the Durango people when they come in."

"I'll do that."

"I would've ordered you a drink if I knew what you like. Buffalo wings are coming." Wade leaned back in the booth. "Did you work all day?"

"This morning. I took the kids to lunch and then to that new superhero movie."

Wade sat up. "We saw it last night. It was okay, but some of the others were better."

"We?"

"Mom and Russ brought the kids to town. They bring them every month or so for a little entertainment. As lovely as Verde and Heaven's Point might be to grow up in, there's not much for a teen and two tweens to do for entertainment."

"I didn't realize you had siblings."

"Yeah. We're a motley crew. Mom raised me from the time I was six and adopted me when I was twelve and she wasn't much more than a kid herself. I was a senior in college when she married Russ, and he's younger than she is. I had the youngest parents at the A and M graduation."

"That couple in the picture with you, in your bookcase. Your mother's gorgeous. So's he." Owen grinned and winked.

"Yeah. The bastard's a looker."

"And the kids?"

"About a year after they married, three siblings were orphaned in San Antonio and became available for adoption. Their birth mother overdosed and their fathers weren't in the picture. Mom and Russ smoked the adoption papers, getting them signed, and never looked back."

"They all had the same mother?"

"Oscar's father was from Reynosa. Melanie's was a Gonzales County redneck, and Jodi's was from Jamaica. Their birth mother's taste in men was... eclectic. The only thing the fathers have in common is that every one of them is a dick."

Their server brought the Buffalo wings and took Owen's order for whiskey on the rocks.

"The kids were lucky to get to stay together. That doesn't always happen. Too often they're separated."

"It almost happened with them. The girls would have gone quickly, but Oscar was more of a problem. He was older, and he had some behaviors issues."

Owen bit into a Buffalo wing. His eyes bulged and he choked a little. "Jesus, that's hot."

Wade handed him his beer. "Drink a little. Wash it down."

Owen took a big swallow of the beer. "So what were some of these less than wonderful behaviors?"

"He was behind in school and acted out because of it. Didn't want to do his homework. Wanted to stay up late. Talked back. He kept stealing food and diapers in the grocery store. It took Mom and

Russ a solid year to convince him that in Verde, folks really prefer that he pay for them."

"Let me guess. He had to take care of himself and his sisters when his birth mother was alive."

"And for a month, after she died out in a field a mile from their trailer park. He was still incensed months later that he and the girls had been taken by CPS. He thought he was taking care of them just fine, thank you very much."

Owen shook his head. "It happens more often than you think. I answered three or four of those calls every year. The things little kids manage to survive, sometimes it blows me away. Did he ever settle down?"

"Took a while, but yeah. He's on grade level and he's doing well. He's definitely a success story, thanks to Mom and Russ."

The waitress brought Owen's drink. The drinks were almost gone and the Buffalo wings were history when Josh walked in with Duke Duncan and a couple of men Wade didn't recognize. Josh's eyes lit up and he made a beeline for the two of them.

"Owen, damn, it's good to see you out. We still owe you for saving our asses that night. I don't know if anyone's told you, but the Navarros were blown away and wrote us the check to prove it." He turned to Wade without a flicker of surprise. "Hey, Wade. It's been a long time. Forty-eight whole hours."

Wade laughed, and Josh motioned his companions over. "I've got some people I want you to meet."

Wade's mouth nearly dropped open. Josh could care less Wade and Owen were out together. And if the expression on Duke's face was anything to go by, he didn't give a damn either.

Josh introduced them to Duke's brother and a young man Wade suspected was Josh's latest sweetie. They squeezed into the booth and pulled up some chairs and shared a round of drinks and gossip about one of their rival theaters. Duke and Josh both expressed their delight that Owen was voicing the book.

"How about an impromptu performance?" Duke teased.

Wade glanced at Owen. "Scene three."

Owen started quoting the book's lines, his rich voice the perfect vehicle to deliver the sage advice.

Wade fell into character and delivered J. Pierrepont's with eager, ambitious enthusiasm. Shivers ran down Wade's back as they ran through the entire exchange. It was the same vibe, the same feel he'd always gotten acting opposite Sandra. Given a few rehearsals, he and Owen would be magic together.

He glanced over at Owen. The light in Owen's eyes told him Owen was feeling the same way.

Josh looked from one to the other. "Damn. That was good. Owen, I don't know what made you have a change of heart, but I thank you from the bottom of mine."

"Hear, hear," Duke said. "You're gonna bring down the house."

"We'll see if anybody feels that way on opening night."

"Oh, they will. You better believe it," Josh promised.

Josh and his companions finished their drinks and wished Wade and Owen a good evening. Wade watched as they left the bar.

"They don't care," he said in wonder. "They don't care one way or another."

"Why should they?" Owen looked at him with amusement. "Wade, every man in that theater knows you're gay. And half the women as well."

Wade gasped. "They do? How?"

"The same way you know. You knew I was, didn't you?"

"I wasn't sure. Not until…"

"Until the gossips filled you in. Or did Letti pitch one of her fits about me?"

"Gossips."

"And I knew you were gay when you checked out my ass that night backstage."

Wade's face flamed. "There might have been some ass-checking going on. So you mean they all knew already?"

"Pretty much. The macho cowboy business only goes so far."

Wade stiffened. "The macho cowboy business is pretty much who I am."

"We know that as well. Lots of macho gay cowboys out there. Ever seen a gay rodeo?"

"Can't say that I have."

"You need to. They're fun." Owen leaned forward. "Man, the two sides of you aren't contradictory. If you'll let them, they'll blend together. There may be gossip around the theater. Or Josh might not even think to mention it. Or he might mention seeing us together, and let people draw their own conclusions. Tonight was the first step. The next step is your family."

"Whoa." Wade held up his hand. "Not gonna happen. What goes at the theater, stays at the theater. I hope."

Owen shook his head. "They need to know."

"No, they don't." He looked at Owen, pleadingly. "Please, let's not fight over it."

Owen's expression softened. "Okay."

Wade smiled softly. "I don't suppose you noticed that they didn't react to your scars, either. Or were you so worried about me that you weren't thinking about their reaction to you?"

Owen grinned sheepishly. "Busted. But they really didn't react. Not like I usually get." He looked around. "This place is getting crowded and those Buffalo wings didn't go far. Want to go someplace for dinner?"

"Sure. Or we can swing back by my place. Russ shot a feral hog, and Mom and Russ filled my freezer with enough pork to last for weeks. We can cook up some of those pork chops."

"You eat feral hog?"

"Sure do, city boy. It's some of the best pork you'll ever put in your mouth."

An hour and a half later, Owen was nodding his head as he looked down at his empty plate.

"Damn. Those were the best pork chops I've ever eaten. How often does your stepdad kill one?"

"This is the third in five years. Russ doesn't actively hunt them, but is more than happy to shoot the ones messing with his grapevines. This one's particularly tasty."

"Everything was delicious. Thanks for cooking."

"I didn't do much." He'd fried the pork chops and toasted some ciabatta to serve alongside a bagged salad. "Did you grow up eating *tamales*?"

"No. We didn't eat much Mexican food. Mom and Dad were completely Americanized. I don't speak Spanish, much to the disgust of my former mother-in-law. You probably ate more *enchiladas* growing up than I did."

"More since I moved here. Verde only had two or three restaurants at any one time, one of which may or may not have been Mexican food. I've really learned to love it here in San Antonio."

They carried their dishes to the kitchen and put their plates in the sink, their arms brushing against each other. Wade sucked in his breath. This close, he could feel the warmth of Owen's body and smell the combination of soap and aftershave, and the unique essence that was Owen.

They turned to face one another, the plates clattering into the sink as they stared into one another's eyes.

"Was tonight only about me coming out? Or was it supposed to be more?" Wade croaked.

Owen reached up and ran his hand down the side of Wade's face. "Of course it was supposed to be more. I'm hot for you. I've had it bad for you since I saw you in that nerdy damn Seymour costume. I can hardly keep my hands off you."

"Then don't," Wade breathed. "Don't keep your hands off me. Touch me all you want."

They lunged at one another. Their lips crashed together. Wade pulled Owen close. He opened his lips and thrust his tongue deep into Owen's mouth. His heart pounded in his throat. Owen's chest was hard, his body hot under the tight tee, and his cock a column of granite beneath his jeans.

Wade could feel his own cock pressing against his zipper, almost to the point of pain. He wanted this man. He wanted to take Owen to bed, to explore his body, to see him in all his naked splendor, and do all the things they could do with and to one another.

He'd wanted it since he laid eyes on the man.

Their breaths mingled as the kiss deepened, Wade's fingers eager as he explored Owen's muscled body and tight ass. He felt Owen's fingers in the hair at his nape. He'd never felt like this in any other man's arms.

It was time for them to take their relationship a step further.

Wade lifted his lips and trailed kisses across Owen's face. His lips touched Owen's scars and Owen flinched.

"Don't do that. Those scars are part of you. There's no reason why I can't kiss them along with the rest of you."

Owen looked up at Wade with a wicked expression on his face. "You want to kiss the rest of me? All of the rest of me?"

Wade laughed out loud. "Oh, yeah. You gonna return the favor?"

"Hell, yeah."

***

He was really going to do it. He and the cowboy were going to get naked.

Owen grabbed Wade by the hand. "Where to?"

Wade pointed to one of two halls leading from the family room. "That way."

Owen yanked Wade's arm and they moved so fast down the hall, they skidded into the master bedroom dominated by a king-sized bed and a huge wall-mounted TV screen. Wade moved to a sturdy armchair where he sat and yanked off one of his boots. Owen sat on the side of the bed and toed off his loafers and yanked off his socks. He stood and shucked his shirt. When his jeans were going down his hips, he heard Wade's sharp gasp. Yeah, the cowboy liked what he saw.

When the rest of Wade's clothes were in a pile next to the chair, they stood facing one another. Owen drank in the breadth of Wade's shoulders, the firm, muscled chest, his washboard abs, his narrow hips, and the enticing package that lay at the juncture of his thighs. His chest was liberally dusted with hair that narrowed into an enticing line down his stomach before flaring to surround his thick, jutting cock. His thighs were powerful and his legs muscular.

Wade reached out and touched Owen's chest. "Do you wax?"

Owen looked down at his bare chest. "God, no. I'm mostly Native American. I have no chest hair, and a sparse beard." He held Wade's hand up to his smooth cheek. "No five o'clock shadow." He ran his fingers through Wade's chest hair. "Not like you hairy Englishmen." He ran his finger around the A&M tattoo. "Real proud of being an Aggie."

"Couldn't be prouder." Wade reached out and touched the intricate pattern of suns, moons and stars running up one side of Owen's chest and up onto his neck. "What's this?"

"Too much tequila on my thirtieth birthday."

Wade chuckled, and ran his hand down Owen's face. "No whisker burn for me." He grinned wickedly and encircled Owen's waist with his arms. "Let's see if I can give you some."

Owen's body sang at the feel of Wade's naked body, their breaths mingling as he lowered his head and laid his lips on Owen's. Their tongues tangled as they fought for dominance, the kiss driving up the pounding in his ribcage. Wade's chest hair tickled Owen's chest and Wade's bristly beard rubbed his cheeks, guaranteeing some whisker burn.

They tumbled onto the bed, and Owen pulled Wade up to face him side-by-side. Wade touched Owen's face, not shying away from the imperfections. Owen touched the thick five o'clock shadow over Wade's jaw, then ran his fingers through Wade's hair, stopping when he encountered a thick surgical scar. He'd ask about it later.

Wade played with Owen's nipples, coaxing them into stiff beads, then tweaking them almost to the point of pain before releasing them, then restarted the delicious torture. Owen slid his hand down Wade's contoured abs and his heart thudded in his ears. His breathing hitched and shivers ran down his back. Damn.

They explored, and Owen savored each touch, squeeze and caress, then gasped when Wade encircled his cock with his big, callused hand and pumped it slowly.

"I love this," Wade breathed. "You. In my hand."

He slid down the bed and pushed Owen's thighs apart. Happy to oblige, he cocked his knees to give Wade more room, then locked his hands behind his head and leaned forward to watch the show.

Wade's tongue danced over the tip of Owen's cock and his lips closed over him. He punched his tongue in the slit, then slid his lips over the head, swirling his tongue around the shaft as he hand-pumped. Owen felt himself grow impossibly harder as he drew closer to the edge. The hand not working his cock teased the juncture of his groin and thigh, and it took everything in him to keep his eyes open. When he thought he couldn't take another minute, Wade cupped his balls and squeezed, sending him spiraling over the edge. His head jerked back as his body quaked, and he shot his load into Wade's mouth.

When his heartbeat slowed, he rasped out, "Fuck."

Wade grinned wickedly.

The little shit knew he had talent. Owen watched as Wade's fingers brushed up and down his abs.

"Give me a minute and I'll return the favor."

"I'm in no hurry." Wade continued to play on Owen's lower stomach before drifting into his pubic hair. "I love your body."

"Not bad for forty-one?"

"Not bad for any age." Wade tugged a handful of pubic hair. "Ready for round two?"

Owen looked at Wade's thick, hard cock. "Oh, yeah."

He sat up and flipped Wade under him, grinning as he lifted his body and made his way down to a cock so swollen its head was purple.

He touched the leaking tip with his finger. "Definitely gorgeous."

"It's a dick, man."

"It's a gorgeous dick. And tonight, it's all mine."

Owen leaned down and swirled his tongue around the tip.

Wade groaned. "Keep that up and I'll come all over you."

"I thought that was the point."

Owen lowered his lips and took Wade into his mouth, loving the earthy, musky taste of him. He wrapped his tongue around the thick, hard cock, reveling in the way it swelled in his mouth. Wade bucked up as Owen sucked hard and deep. He gasped and erupted into Owen's throat. Owen didn't relent as Wade thrashed and groaned and jet after jet pulsed into his mouth. He didn't lift his head until Wade's cock started to deflate.

Wade sank back with an embarrassed expression. "Sorry I blew so fast," he murmured.

"Why are you apologizing? Total rush knowing I turn you on like that."

"Some guys don't like it when I come that fast. And the few times I did a girl, they really didn't like it."

Owen stretched out beside Wade. "I'm not some guy. And I'm sure as hell not a girl. If you want to go off like a rocket, be my guest."

"But later? When I'm inside you?"

"Don't stress it." Owen laid his hand over Wade's swelling cock. "You're already recovering. Ah, to be young again."

Owen wrapped his hand around Wade's dick, coaxing it from half-mast to fully swollen. Wade made humming noises as Owen pumped with one hand while working Wade's balls with the other. Wade writhed as his hips thrust high and hard, before exploding, his come shooting jets onto his stomach.

Wade sank into the mattress, his breaths coming in ragged gasps. Owen moved out of bed to the bathroom where he washed his hands then found a washcloth, wet it and soaped it up. He returned to the bed and cleaned the come from Wade's cock and stomach. He threw the washcloth on the floor, and Wade sat up in bed, legs crossed.

Owen jerked his chin toward Wade's arm. "What happened?"

"An accident when I was a kid. Same one that got me this." He pointed to the back of his head. "The ones on my leg are from a football injury." He changed the subject quickly. "You hungry? I have ice cream in the freezer."

"Nah." Owen pointed to the big screen. "Why here? Most people put the big screen in the family room."

"So I could bring my lovers here and not disturb Sandra and Noelle."

"Who?"

"Sandra and her daughter Noelle. She was my roomie for over three years. We did a bunch of plays together. She was the only one who knew about me, besides the men I slept with."

"I think Sophie might've said something about her. The woman who went back to her husband in Tennessee."

"Yeah."

"Why did you come out to her?"

"I had to since we were gonna live together. We never explained our relationship, and let everyone think what they wanted to."

"A beard," Owen muttered.

Wade dipped his head. "I miss her. I miss them both."

"I'm sure you do. But now you can live the life you were meant to live."

Wade stiffened. Then the cheeky grin returned. "Popcorn and a little TV?"

He reached into the nightstand, pulled out a box of condoms and a tube of lube, and lifted a brow.

Owen laughed. "Oh, yeah. Popcorn and TV."

CHAPTER 7

Owen slitted his eyes open and peered into the dim light of early morning. The room was mostly dark but for thin strips of pink light filtering through wooden slates. A hard, muscular arm was thrown across his stomach, and soft breathing teased the hair at his nape. Owen's body ached deliciously and he hadn't felt this sated in a long time, if ever.

The sheets were tangled and the room smelled of sex. Used condoms littered the floor and the tube of lube lay uncapped on the nightstand. They'd made popcorn and Owen had introduced Wade to the real-life murder mysteries on Discovery ID before introducing his dick to the inside of Wade's body. Usually, he topped, but Wade wanted more, and everything they did to each other felt so damned good, Owen relented and let Wade in.

Sometime after two in the morning, they'd finally turned off the light and curled into each other, their bodies spent.

He eased out of bed, went to the bathroom and emptied his bladder. With a quick search of the medicine cabinet, he was able to locate some eye drops to clean the area around his prosthetic eye. He returned to the bedroom and sat in the ugly corner armchair and studied Wade.

They'd definitely taken their relationship to another level. Last night hadn't been a one-off. They'd be back in one of their beds soon and often.

Wade murmured something in his sleep and turned over. Asleep, he looked younger and more relaxed. Awake, the guard he maintained drew his body taut, the message clear—*stay back, I've got secrets and you're not invited to ask about them.* That strain showed to those who knew to look for it. Unfortunately, Wade had been living his lie his whole life, so most people didn't have a clue they were seeing a front and not the real man.

The sad part was there was absolutely no reason for Wade to live like that. Maybe his stress level would drop now that he'd come out to the Durango crowd. That had been a huge step forward.

The next step would be his family. They needed to know.

Owen rubbed the knot between his eyes. There was always the danger of rejection. Many families did that. But he sensed from the picture Wade had painted of Angie and Russ Riley, they would be the last two people to do that. But even if they were unhappy, even if Angie rejected her son, it would still be better for Wade in the long run if he was honest with himself about himself. The stress of hiding from the world was going to take a serious toll on him if he kept it up.

Owen's stomach rumbled and he yawned. Wade's kitchen was well-stocked. Maybe he would enjoy breakfast in bed, courtesy of his new lover. He pulled on his boxer briefs and wandered to the kitchen, poking into the refrigerator and the cabinets. Eggs. Bacon. Bread to make toast. Nothing fancy, but it would refuel them for another round in Wade's bed. He used Wade's fancy coffeemaker to make them each a latte, and was on his way to Wade's bedroom when Wade cried out in his sleep, "Grandma, no. You can't mean it."

Owen set the coffee mugs on the kitchen counter and rushed to the bedroom. Wade was sweating and thrashing, deep in some hellish nightmare. Owen took him by the shoulders and coaxed in a steady voice, "Wade. Wake up."

Still deep in terror, Wade brushed Owen's hands away. "No, Mom." He continued to murmur under his breath.

Owen took Wade's shoulders more firmly this time and gave them a shake. "Wake up, Wade. It's only a nightmare."

Wade blinked and his eyes snapped open. He looked around, confused for a minute. Then he looked at Owen and his face turned a deep shade of red.

"Sorry about that. Did I wake you?"

"No. I was making coffee in the kitchen. What in the hell were you dreaming about?"

Wade's eyes shuttered, his face became a mask of stone.

"Nothing."

"It wasn't 'nothing.' You were yelling 'no' to your mother and your grandmother."

Wade shrugged. "Something from a long time ago. It's not worth talking about." Owen took a breath and was about to argue when Wade shook his head.

"I'd much rather concentrate on today and the coffee I smell." His whole expression pleaded with Owen to back off. "Please. Let's focus on today. That's what's important."

Owen clamped his lips shut and nodded. He didn't agree with Wade one damn bit. Whatever he was dreaming about was significant. But he couldn't force Wade to confide if he didn't want to.

When Owen returned with their coffee, Wade was sitting up, leaning against the headboard.

"I didn't know how you like your coffee. If you want, I can go get sugar and cream."

Wade took the mug from Owen's outstretched hand. "No, this is perfect."

Owen sat at the end of the bed, and they sipped their coffee in silence for a while before he asked, "How ya feel about coming out last night to the Durango?"

"Okay, I guess. I'll get a better idea when I see what the reaction is on Tuesday."

"That's not what I asked. How do *you* feel about it?"

"Fine. Maybe a little more relaxed knowing I don't have to worry if I do or say something in front of them and give myself away."

"Good. That's how you're supposed to feel. So when are you going to take the next step?"

Wade stiffened beside him. "What next step?"

"Telling your family."

Wade turned to him, his eyes shuttered again. "That's off the table. Completely." He slid out of bed and headed to the bathroom.

Owen followed him. "Why? Why is telling your mom and her husband the truth scary?"

Wade whirled around with fire in his eyes. "Why is it so damned important to you? I don't comment on what you do with your family. What in the hell gives you the right to mouth off about mine? What I say to them is my own damn business and no one else's." He slammed the bathroom door in Owen's face.

Owen yanked the door open and pointed to the bed. "That's what gives me the right."

"How does us fucking give you the right to weigh in on my family?" He slammed the door again.

Owen's fingers trembled as he gathered up his clothes and pulled on his jeans, shirt and shoes. His mind raced, trying to find the right thing to say to make Wade understand how corrosive the secrecy was. He was putting together an argument when Wade stalked out and grabbed a pair of boxer briefs from the drawer. He pulled them on, gracing Owen with a glare as he did.

"Wade."

"Drop it. I mean it, man."

"Damn it. Listen to me. The secrecy is eating you alive. You're tense and on-guard every damn minute of your life. You've already taken the first step with your Durango friends. Why is it so different coming out to your family?"

Wade glared, the muscles in his jaw jumping in time to the blood pumping wildly in his neck.

"Because I don't want them to know how ugly I am."

Owen reared back like he'd been gut punched. "Fuck. Me. You think because you're gay, you're ugly? What we shared last night was ugly? That I'm *ugly*?"

"They would think that. You don't get it. You didn't grow up in small town Texas. You grew up on the west coast, near San Francisco for fuck's sake, and studied acting around open-minded theater people. I love my family, and I love the people of Verde. But they're so far from your experience I can't even describe how they think. My family would think I'm ugly. My old friends in Verde sure as hell would."

"What about you? What do you think?"

Wade's silence spoke volumes.

"Fuck this. I'll be damned if I get involved with a man who's too chickenshit to be himself. Who thinks what we shared last night was ugly. Who thinks gay is ugly. Who thinks I'm ugly." His throat closed and he could barely speak. "Ya know, it's a fucking shame. We could've had something special."

"Yeah, we could have." Wade's voice was hard. "As long as I do things your way."

Owen clamped his mouth shut. Wade could have the last word. Owen stuffed his wallet and keys in his pocket and marched out of the house, slammed his car into gear, and squealed his tires backing out of the driveway.

Fuckin' hell. Last night had been the best damn sex of his life.

***

Wade pulled his truck into the parking lot behind the Durango. Someone had unlocked the back door, saving everyone a hike around the block. He was late, thanks to a last-minute meeting with the district engineer. The lot was full for rehearsal night. He hotfooted it into the theater and cut through the side door to the Academy rehearsal rooms, dreading the inevitable. Owen would be here tonight. He'd started late and already missed a couple weeks of rehearsal. Aubrey would want them to rehearse J. Pierrepont's scenes reading the book. Wade wondered how it would be working with Owen after fucking their brains out on Saturday night, then crashing and burning on Sunday morning. He hoped to hell they could still pull off the magic they'd had in the bar. He hoped they could put their personal feelings aside.

He'd not seen or heard from Owen since the man had stormed out. He'd been furious, with good reason. Wade had never meant that he found Owen ugly, or that he found homosexuality ugly. Unfortunately, that was exactly how things had come out.

But Wade was pissed, too. Owen had no idea where he was coming from or why he felt the way he did. But the blowup had forced Wade to do some serious soul-searching. He'd taken a hard look at himself and his feelings. He didn't think homosexuality was ugly. He didn't think what he'd done with Owen Saturday night was ugly. And he sure as hell didn't think Owen Aldrete was ugly.

But Wade Baxter was one ugly son of a bitch.

He ran his hand down the side of his face, again hearing the words that haunted him for the last five years. *"You're a damn queer?"* his former best friend, Benny Keller, had sneered at him. *"You're standing here telling me you're a fucking queer? You're as fucked up and ugly as the rest of the Baxters. You're a fucking bad lot, every damn one of you. You just picked a different brand of fucked up and ugly."*

Then Benny had broken his nose.

He'd tried not to take Benny's words to heart, but Benny had been his best friend since the second grade. They'd seen each other through so much. Every word Benny had uttered that afternoon had been a knife in his heart. And knowing how Benny reacted, Wade understood how the rest of Verde would feel. Under no circumstances was he willing to take the chance to find out how his mom and Russ would react.

Wade made his way into the Academy rooms, where rehearsals were being held. To his surprise, rather than having him work with Owen, Aubrey had him and Lester Parker, the distinguished older actor playing J.B. Biggley, rehearse the "Grand Old Ivy" scene. Lester taught with Letti at the community college, and was as talented as they came. Nevertheless, it took them most of the evening to get the scene down to Aubrey's specifications, and she said it was too late to rehearse another scene.

"Be on time for next rehearsal." She nailed Wade with a pointed look.

Wade started toward the door.

"Don't mind Aubrey." Letti fell into step beside him and they headed out. "She's been on a tear all evening."

"I wasn't planning to lay awake tonight worrying about it."

She turned to him with speculation in her eyes. "So you're Owen's chickenshit nobody."

Wade's eyes narrowed as he turned to her. "What did he say?"

"Absolutely nothing. I don't discuss his love life with him. I discuss as little with him as I can manage. But it's pretty damn easy to connect the dots, you and Owen out on a date a week after he made the crack. I guess you kissed and made up."

"And your point would be?" he snapped.

"Whoa. Put a lid on the mad. Look, I've made no secret of the way I feel about Owen. A whole lot of people on Team Owen think I'm a vindictive bitch. Maybe I am. But Owen's a cheater. Plain and simple. I'm trying to warn you." She put her hand on Wade's arm. "I think the world of you. I always have. I don't want you to get hurt. Especially if you're just now navigating the waters of a gay love life."

"I've been navigating the waters of a gay love life for years," Wade said dryly. "I've learned the rules by now."

"Okay, then," she said doubtfully.

"And at the risk of getting my ass in trouble with you big-time, cut him a little slack. Owen probably fought his true nature for years. He lived as a straight man until he was what? Thirty-five? From what everybody has said, he was a good husband for most of the marriage. I think he deserves a little credit for that."

"Tough shit. Cut him some slack, my ass. Cheating is cheating. He made vows and he broke them. He was unfaithful. Doesn't matter if it was a guy or a girl. I don't give a damn what his true nature is, and I don't think he deserves one damned bit of credit for anything. Bottom line, Owen cheated on me. Period. End of statement."

Wade raised his eyebrow. "What about you? Weren't you cheating on him at the same time? Weren't you as guilty as he was?"

She flinched and tears filled her eyes. *"One time,"* she snarled as she nailed Wade with a tearful glare. "One damned night, and I've felt shitty about it ever since. You tell me how that compares to months and months of him fucking Johnny Roberts in every motel in this city." Tears dripped down her cheeks, and she turned on her heel and ran out of the building.

"Jesus. I wish I'd kept my damn mouth shut."

"You probably should have."

Wade jumped and turned around. Owen was back in his signature ball cap pulled low on his forehead. Wade took in that damn-near perfect body and remembered what it looked like minus the tee shirt and jeans. His mouth watered and he felt himself start to harden. Reminding himself he was pissed-off didn't lessen his desire to jump Owen's bones and have his way with the delectable man.

"What was I supposed to say? She was trash-mouthing you, under the guise of 'warning' me about your propensity to cheat."

Owen shrugged. "I did cheat on her. In her mind, that's worse than divorcing her."

"Why cheat? Why didn't you just leave?"

Owen gestured toward the back door and they walked down the hall together.

"At that point, I was trying to have eat my cake and have it too. I was naïve to think I could stay in my marriage and enjoy being gay on the side. Stupid of me."

"Why did you want to stay in the marriage if you loved Johnny?"

Owen laughed. "I didn't love Johnny. I lusted after him. Big difference." He stopped and turned to Wade. "I tried to keep the marriage together because I loved Letti. I loved that woman with all my heart."

"Huh? I don't get it."

They started walking again. "Being gay doesn't stop a man from loving a woman, especially the mother of his children. Some would say I'm bisexual. I was married, and for a long time I managed a routine of an unspectacular sex life. The sight of a pretty woman will still turn my head. But as time passed, I wanted sex with Letti less and less, and sex with men more and more. That's when I tried keeping my marriage intact and have my life as a gay man on the side. Which was completely and totally unfair to Letti. She has every right to be pissed about it."

He paused, stopped, then resumed walking. "As much as I enjoy being out of the closet, living the life I was meant to live, my greatest regret is that I couldn't be the husband Letti needed. I'll feel shitty about that until I go to my grave. She deserved better, especially after she got pregnant and chose to give up her dreams of Hollywood, and give me Sophie instead. I hate that I hurt her so badly. I hate that it left her so bitter. I wish with all my heart for her to find someone who can make her happy."

"Does she date?"

A small smile touched Owen's lips. "As hot as Carmela Lopez is to marry off her divorced daughter, I'm sure there are blind dates up one side and down the other. I don't know if anything ever comes of them. Between the theater, the kids, and her teaching job, Letti stays busy."

They walked out the door and Owen followed Wade to his truck. Wade unlocked the door and started to get in, but Owen put his hand on Wade's arm.

"I could do better by you than I did Letti, if you'd let me. But you have to decide whether or not to let me. The ball's in your court."

"I know that." Wade shut the truck's door and leaned against the side of the pickup. "What I was trying to say Sunday morning when I made you so mad...I made a hash of it. What I was trying to say and what came out of my mouth were two different things. I've had some time to think about things a little. Put some things into perspective."

Owen leaned on the truck, mirroring Wade's pose. "What conclusions did you come to?"

"Gay is not ugly. What we shared was about as far from ugly as anyone could get." He picked up Owen's hand and kissed it. "And you're sure as hell not ugly."

"So what about you?" Owen asked, softly. "If my memory serves, the whole thing started when you said you didn't want your family to know how ugly you were. Is being gay why you feel ugly?"

"Not really. But it's why I don't want Mom to know about it. She's had too much ugliness in her life. The kind of ugliness I don't talk about. For years, I was the only bright spot in her life, and I'm still a source of her happiness. I don't want her to feel her bright spot isn't so bright."

"Would she really be all that disappointed?"

"I'm afraid she would. I don't want to take that chance."

Owen looked at him, curiously. "What is it that makes you feel so ugly if it's not being gay?"

Wade sighed. A part of him longed to share the Baxter family secrets with this man. But another part of him warned him to keep his mouth shut. If Owen knew the truth about him, knew exactly how fucked up the Baxter family was, he'd run for the hills.

"Things, Owen. Really fucked-up things better left unsaid."

Owen looked at him, skeptically. "I'm supposed to be okay with that?"

"I hope you will be." Wade turned and took Own by the shoulders. "Please. Don't make me rehash it. I'm trying to move on, not dwell on things I can't change."

"If you say so. For the time being. But at some point, if this relationship goes where I hope it does, you're going to have to level with me."

"At some point, I will. In the meantime, please be patient with me."

Owen's passionate kiss was all the answer Wade needed.

***

Owen leaned against the wall and watched Lester and Letti rehearse a scene between J.B. Biggley and Hedi LaRue. Lester and Letti had enormous chemistry on stage, perhaps because they shared an office in the community college drama department and were the best of friends.

Tonight, they were having the time of their lives putting together one of the funnier scenes between the CEO of Worldwide Wickets and the seductive cigarette girl turned inept secretary. Letti was a born comedienne with perfect timing and the right amount of sexy snark to breathe life into Hedi.

Owen watched them for a few minutes and then wandered to the next rehearsal room, where Wade was running through dialogue with the actor playing Twimble, the head of the Worldwide Wickets mailroom. As the eager, ambitious J. Pierrepont Finch, Wade was in his element, playing a character that was handsome, charming, and destined to get the girl. Which was ironic, but not uncommon. Gay men, including superstars in Hollywood, played romantic leads all the time. A lot of leading men hid their homosexuality from the world.

Owen ought to know. He'd done it for years.

Aubrey had indicated she wanted him and Wade to work together this evening, so he sat on a folding chair in the lobby and pulled out his phone and tried to ignore the way the young ensemble dancer sitting across from him stared at his marred face. It wasn't like she could see all that much. His ball cap was low enough to hide part of it, and the rest was in shadows.

He'd tried a few times coming to rehearsal without a hat or a hoodie, but the startled looks and stares of the young cast and crew cut him to the bone and drove him to put his disguise back on. He'd been okay in the darkened bar that evening. But the beautiful Durango crowd wasn't ready for the real Owen any time soon. This bunch was simply too pretty to take his scarring in stride.

He'd gone through his personal email and was about to call up his reading app when Wade poked his head in the door. "Aubrey's ready for us."

Owen followed Wade down to an empty rehearsal room. Everyone in the cast would be glad when next week the sets would be finished and they were rehearsing on-stage. They would have two weeks of stage rehearsal before the show opened the Friday after Thanksgiving.

Everyone else involved with the production would be there every night for the two weeks leading up to opening night. Each night they'd layer in another part of the production until it all came together during dress rehearsal. That final rehearsal was in some ways more important than opening night. Especially since that was the evening the newspaper critics came and gave them thumbs-up or down.

Owen's heart beat a little faster in anticipation. He'd always loved those two weeks, despite the fatigue and pressure, as months of scene-by-scene work came together a piece at a time. He enjoyed seeing how each layer added a new dimension to the production. He loved the adrenalin buzz of waiting backstage for the curtain to sweep toward the wings on opening night. He loved it all. He'd missed it so much.

He and Wade ran through the first scene under Aubrey's critical eye. Owen would be standing offstage, but close enough so that he could see Wade, as J. Pierrepont Finch, "reading" the book.

A smile played around Aubrey's lips as they finished their third run-through. "Josh is right. Y'all are magic together." She cocked her head. "Wouldn't I love to see you two play Georges and Albin, in *La Cage aux Folles*."

Wade looked startled. "Birdcage? Us?"

Owen snickered. "Which one of us gets to be Robin Williams?"

"I like the musical version better," Aubrey said.

"So do I," they said in unison.

Aubrey told them to run through it a couple more times, and wandered off. Wade and Owen looked at one another.

"Word's definitely out," Wade said.

"Seems so. So you want Georges or Albin?"

Wade looked in the rehearsal room mirror, turning this way and that. "Ya think I'd look good in drag?"

Owen looked down at Wade's sneakers. "We'd have to special-order the boots. Maybe we could even do *Kinky Boots* with you in a pair of size fourteens."

Wade looked down at Owen's booted feet. "You, on the other hand, could probably find a pair at the mall. Could you walk in them?" Owen took a few prancing steps, swinging his hips like a woman. "Albin it is then. I'll be Georges."

"It's not my feet I'd be worried about." Owen sighed. "It's good to be back. But it sucks that I'll be forever stuck in offstage roles."

Wade opened his mouth and shut it.

Probably better that way, Owen thought. He was no mood for another of Wade's your-face-isn't-that-bad pep talks. He'd already had three of those from his young lover and didn't want to have to listen to a fourth.

Aubrey came by a few minutes later. She heard them one more time and told them to blow the joint. A cool November wind ruffled Owen's hair as they walked to their parked vehicles.

"Your place or mine?" Wade asked.

"You got any lube or condoms left?"

"Crap. I haven't had time to go by the pharmacy."

"Then my place it is."

Traffic was unusually heavy for a Friday night, and progress was slow on the major artery leading to Owen's apartment. He started growing hard as he followed Wade's pickup down the busy streets.

They'd gone home together the night of Wade's set-to with Letti, and had scorched the sheet for hours. They'd spent a lot of nights together since, their passion burning bright as they got to know each other's bodies top to bottom.

But it hadn't all been about sex. They'd cooked meals together. Wade had memorized lines or worked on DOT stuff while Owen managed his webpages. They'd gone to a couple more blow-em-ups, and again made it a game to catch the errors.

They'd gone downtown for drinks and dinner on the Riverwalk, enjoying the gay and straight bars. And they'd spent a couple of late nights at Thirties, laughing and talking and savoring time spent with their friends at the Durango.

Wade and Owen pulled into the apartment's lot and parked side by side. They raced up the stairs and Owen dropped his key twice. Wade grabbed the keys and got the door open, slammed it shut, and pressed Owen against it, nipping and sucking, their tongues warring to be in control.

"Damn," Wade rasped when they finally came up for air. "It keeps gettin' better."

"And it's gonna be a whole lot better in about five minutes." Owen grabbed Wade by the hand and pulled him toward the bedroom. "Lube and condoms are in there."

Stripped bare, Wade pushed Owen down on the bed, touching, kissing, licking, and stroking. He inserted a lubed finger first, and then another, moving them in and out until Owen's body was ready. Slowly, he entered him from behind.

Owen's body welcomed Wade, his young lover's cock easing into him. His own cock twitched, and pleasure flooded his body as Wade pumped hard and fast, his hand stroking Owen's cock. Wade's breathing became gasps before he stiffened and cried out, tremors shaking the man's body as he came.

After a few moments, his breathing even out and he pulled out slowly, and then threw the condom on the floor.

"Lemme finish you."

"In a minute." Owen turned to face his lover, kissing him hard while his hands traveled Wade's strong, hard body.

In some ways, the build-up was as satisfying as the act itself, as Owen readied Wade's body for the ultimate intimacy. He touched and stroked, and Wade began to harden again.

Owen sat up and ran his fingers down Wade's stiffening cock. "I take it this means you're ready for me."

"You would be right."

With a gasp of pleasure, Owen entered Wade's willing warmth. His cock swelled in the tight, wet. He thrust slowly at first, savoring the tease, but soon he was moving faster, lost in the sensation of Wade's talented mouth, pulling his orgasm out of him. He threw back his head and cried out harshly as his body erupted in an explosion of pure, white-hot delight, radiating out from his core to the tips of his fingers and toes.

He collapsed, and Wade joined him, his chest heaving and his breathing ragged.

"Damn, man, that was—"

They jumped at the pounding coming from the other side of the wall.

"Oops," Wade said, his eyes dancing with devilment. "I take it your neighbor's not as thrilled as we are. Tight-assed prudes?"

Owen lifted himself and rolled off Wade. "She probably has to work tomorrow. I'll get her a box of candy at the grocery store."

They sat up, their arms around one another.

"Got anything to eat? I didn't have time before rehearsal," Wade said.

"Not a damned thing. I'll get some clothes on and go to that drive-thru taco place."

Owen threw on minimum clothing and was back in ten minutes. They killed the food, then watched a little TV before coming together again for another round that was slower and quieter, but no less passionate. Wade gathered Owen into his arms and was soon snoring lightly in Owen's ear.

He snuggled down beside his cowboy and threw his arm across Wade's stomach. He was tired, full, and sated. All of which should have made sleep come easy. But Owen lay awake in the dark, staring across the room at the streetlight outlined faintly behind the curtains.

Damn. He was falling in love with this troubled man, and he wasn't sure it was a good idea. Wade had yet to open up. While there had been no more nightmares, on several occasions Wade had zoned out, but never talked about what took him far away. The man harbored some big secrets, and as close as they had become, Owen could tell Wade was no closer to sharing them than he'd been before, and they never discussed Wade's refusal to level with his family.

Owen shut his eyes and snuggled closer to Wade's warm chest.

He hoped the continuing secrecy wasn't a sign that his affection wasn't reciprocated.

***

Owen opened his eyes and looked around his bedroom. Wade's side of the bed was empty, and he could hear the television in the living room and smell coffee. He stumbled into the bathroom, did his thing, and then pulled on his boxers and found Wade peering into the refrigerator.

"You may keep plenty of lube and condoms, but your food stash leaves a lot to be desired," Wade observed.

"Hey, I got spoiled having a wife to do most of the cooking. I'm the king of the fast food."

"Yeah. I miss Sandra's cooking, too."

They looked at one another.

"We either hit the drive-in for more tacos, or go somewhere for a real meal," Wade said.

"What about the brunch over at the steakhouse? No, wait. All you have are last night's clothes."

"Well, I might have a couple of things in a duffel in the truck." Wade's eyes danced.

Owen laughed. "I have a duffel in mine, too, in case we ended up at your place."

They shared a long shower, soaping one another's bodies with fingers slick with shampoo, and stroking one another's cocks to a shared climax that had them both gasping.

They dressed and hopped in Wade's truck together. The steakhouse buffet was busy and they were waiting for a table when a small boy streaked across the lobby and threw his arms around Wade's knees.

"Uncle Wade!" The child laughed and clung to Wade's long legs.

Wade looked at the child with astonishment before his face broke into a gentle smile.

"Jace, darlin', how are you?" He picked up the child so Jace could give him a hug.

At that moment, a frazzled-looking redhead came barreling through the crowd.

"Jace? Sweetie, where did you run off to?" She spotted Wade holding the little boy. Her face split into a smile and she skidded to a stop. "Oh, you found your Uncle Wade. How are you, honey?" She engulfed Wade in a huge hug.

Wade hugged the woman as the crowd parted again and a tall man carrying an even younger child strode through. The man seemed totally oblivious to the stares and winces he drew from those around him.

"I see you found our little renegade." He shook Wade's hand. "How ya doin', buddy? Getting all those bridges built?"

"Sure am. Getting all those cars sold?"

"Number one in the state last month. We were there 'til midnight, most nights. Emily's glad the sale's over so I can come home once in a while."

Emily and Jason Donahue. Wade's friends from college.

Owen glanced over at Wade. His lover looked at him, uncertainly. He wondered what Wade would do. He supposed he could melt away in the crowd until the Donahues moved on, but he'd be damned if he let Wade marginalize him like that. He would introduce himself if he had to.

Before he had to do that, Wade turned to him. "Owen, this is Emily and Jason Donahue. Jason and I were college roommates. Emily lived next door and had the unfortunate taste to marry this ugly bastard. Later, her brother had the excellent taste to marry my mom. My man here is Jace. The squirt Jason's holding is Riley. Emily, Jason, this is Owen Aldrete. He acts with me at the Durango."

He acts with me at the Durango? At least Wade introduced him, which was more than Owen expected.

But in all fairness, he didn't know how Wade could have introduced him. There were no good words to describe what they were to one another, but "My man" would've done nicely.

Not that Wade would have used it.

They chatted a few minutes before the hostess called their name.

"Why don't you see how big the table is," Emily suggested. "We could share a table and get caught up. If that would be all right? We haven't seen Wade in forever."

Wade looked like a deer in the headlights. Owen wondered if he would make some bullshit excuse, but to his credit he spoke to the hostess. There was a larger table being bussed that would fit them all. Owen's lips twitched as Emily kept looking at him, curiously, and then to her husband, with a knowing gleam. The sweet-faced redhead was trying to figure it out. Her scarred husband already knew the score.

Brunch was going to be interesting.

CHAPTER 8

Wade cursed the sweat forming on his forehead. God Almighty, of all the people in the world they could have run into, Emily and Jason. Of all his old friends, it had to be the two that were closest to his family. No, they were family. His mom was married to her brother. It had to be the two who would be the most likely to share his secret with his mom.

If they figured it out.

He glanced over at Jason and groaned inwardly at the speculation in his friend's eyes. Jason already was on to them. If Emily didn't put two and two together, Jason would do the math for her.

Wade was completely and totally screwed.

The hostess returned with a stack of menus. They fell in line and weaved their way through the crowded restaurant, past the steaming buffet tables, to a big round table in the back. Their hostess replaced two of the chairs with highchairs, and Jason waved them all toward the buffet, volunteering to wait with the kids until Emily came back.

"Say, why don't Wade and I go through with you while you make plates for the boys?" We'll take them to the table and go back for our own," Owen suggested.

"Good thinking," Emily said. "Thanks."

"Tag-teaming in a buffet. Brings back memories. We used to do it all the time when my children were young."

Emily looked more confused than ever.

They followed her while she made the children's plates. Owen spirited the food to the table. The three of them made their own plates and relieved Jason, who was patiently cutting up a pancake for Riley. Wade wondered what the hell they were going to talk about, but Emily was occupied with feeding the children, and was busy with them until Jason returned with a plate stacked high and slid in next to Owen.

"I love the buffet," Jason said. "It's the only place I can fill up and not spend a fortune." He smiled.

Owen made a production of eyeing Jason. "I gotta admit, not too many dudes make Wade look small."

"Amazingly, of the three of us who roomed together at A and M, Wade was the smallest. He still is. Benny was as big as me then, and he's put on a ton since he graduated. And I've gained my share. Unlike Wade here, who's managed to stay college-fit. Wade, how big had Benny gotten the last time you saw him?"

"I... I haven't seen him in a while," Wade stammered.

"You haven't?" Emily piped up. "I thought you two were close."

He felt his face flame. "Not as close as we used to be. With him being out of state these days."

At least he hoped Benny was still out of state. He had no idea where Benny was.

Emily started to say something, but Owen jumped in.

"Wade tells me you're a dynamite car salesman, Jason. Do you enjoy dealing with customers?"

Thank you, Owen.

"Love it, most days. It gives me a chance to do what I do best. Schmooze with other people."

"And make money. Jason's *real* good at doing that." Wade couldn't resist the teasing comment.

"Hey, I don't make money off everybody I schmooze with."

"Most of them you do." Emily's eyes twinkled. "Actually, Owen, we're just giving Jason a hard time. He really does love being around people. And people love being around him."

Owen looked at Jason for a minute. "Can I ask a question?"

Jason nodded. "From the decoration on your face I doubt you put there willingly, I bet I know what it is. Yeah, it was hard at first putting myself out there and hearing the gasps and seeing the stares and having the occasional little kid run the other direction. But I wanted to do the job badly enough that I put myself out there anyway. I wanted to live life badly enough that I got over it. It's like this. If I was going to have the life my woman and I share, if I was going to be around people and live my life to the fullest, it meant getting over other people's reaction to the scarring and giving them a chance to get to know me. And buy something, if I could persuade them to do it." He winked.

"How the hell do you get past it?" Owen persisted. "The gasps and the stares?"

Jason tipped his chin toward Owen. "How'd you get hurt?"

"Trying to defuse a bomb."

"You were a cop?" Jason asked. "Did you have to take a medical retirement?"

"I did. It cost me my job and my hobby acting in community theater. I'm a webpage designer now. I don't have to face the public looking like this."

"So you got hurt saving other people's lives. How often do you remind yourself of that?"

"Not often enough," Wade stated.

"It was no big deal," Owen murmured.

"It was a big deal," Emily insisted. "Jason runs a support group for wounded warriors that you might want to attend. It would help you get past some of the self-consciousness. It helped Jason and every hero in the group."

"Oh, but I'm not a hero. Far from it," Owen objected. "Those wounded soldiers, they're heroes. Not me."

"I beg to differ," Jason said firmly. "You are a hero, even if you don't feel like one. It helps sitting down with others in the same boat as you. I promise. We talk about everything, including the scars that don't show."

Wade flinched. Maybe he should join Jason's group.

"I don't know."

Jason whipped out his wallet and handed Owen a card. "We meet on Tuesday evening at the dealership. Coffee, cookies, and a lot of understanding. If nothing else, you can share some fresh war stories with us. Ours are getting old. We'll be looking for you."

Wade laughed. "And here we have the presumptive close Jason is so good at." He reached out under the table and squeezed Owen's hand. "At least think about it." Owen squeezed back.

Wade turned his attention to Emily. "We haven't heard from you. How's school going?"

Emily launched into a story about one of the undergraduate classes she was teaching, and then he and Owen told them about *How to Succeed*. As breakfast continued, Wade felt himself start to relax a little. Maybe he was wrong. Maybe Jason hadn't caught on. Maybe Emily wouldn't.

Maybe it would be all right after all.

Wade finished his third cup of coffee. "Damn. I need to make a restroom run. Be back in a second."

He handed Owen a twenty and went to the restroom, hoping to make it back to the table before anyone left. But Emily was waiting for him outside the men's room. Her arms were folded in front of her, and she wasn't smiling.

"What is Owen to you?" she demanded.

"We're good friends," he said through stiff lips.

"So are Jason and I. You didn't answer my question. *What is Owen to you?*"

"If you're asking if I slept in his bed last night, the answer is yes," Wade snapped.

Emily reared back as though he'd slapped her. "Why in the hell didn't you ever say something?" she asked. "Why did you let me make a fool of myself all this time trying to fix you up with my friends?"

"I wasn't trying to make a fool of you," Wade protested. "I tried to discourage you."

"You could have said something," she said bitterly. "A simple, 'Emily, I'm not into women' would have done it. Instead, you let me go on trying to fix you up with a parade of them." The hurt in her eyes made him feel guilty. "What about Sandra? Did she know?"

"We lived together for three years. Of course she knew."

"What about Benny?"

"He knows." Wade couldn't keep the bitterness out of his voice.

"So you could tell Sandra and Benny but not me. How do you think that makes me feel?"

"Damn it, Emily. Benny is why I never told you. The son of a bitch threw me out of the apartment and broke my nose. He hasn't spoken to me since. I was scared. I thought you'd hate me the way Benny does." He hung his head. "I'd lost Benny. I couldn't lose you, too."

"You wouldn't have lost me. What kind of person do you think I am?"

"After Benny acted the way he did, I didn't know. I thought he'd understand, and he didn't. And then Russ married my mom, and you and Jason became family. At that point, I was sure I couldn't tell you."

"What difference does it make that we're now family? I don't get it."

"Think about it, Emily. Think about the Baxters. Think about the ugliness they put my mother through. Do you really think I want more of the Baxter ugliness contaminating my mother's life? I'm not real proud, you know."

Emily stared at him. "I don't know what to say."

"I'll tell you what you can say. Nothing. Absolutely nothing. You can promise me that you and Jason will never breathe a single solitary word about me to anyone in the Riley family. Mom, Russ, Gran and Gramps, Holly and Jimmy…none of them need to know. Because if one of them knows, the rest will find out. I don't want to do that to Mom. Please."

She shook her head. "Whatever."

Wade gulped when Emily's eyes filled with tears. "Aw, honey, no. Don't cry. Please."

She turned on her heel and left. Wade slumped against the wall, looking up at the sound of clapping from the end of the hall.

"Way to go, champ. You hurt that woman big-time," Owen jeered.

"You think I don't know that?" Wade ground out. "Let's get out of here."

They walked in tense silence to the truck, and were halfway back to Owen's before he spoke.

"I'm tired of you being ashamed," he said tensely. "I'm tired of your hating yourself for being gay."

"There's not much I can do about it. Besides, I've already said it's not because I'm gay. I have plenty of other reasons not to like myself."

"I'm getting a little tired of that shit, too. You're not making sense."

"Since when do feelings make sense?"

Owen was silent for a moment. "What the hell do you have to hate yourself about? You're young, good-looking, talented, and have the world by the tail. You have no reason not to like yourself."

"Oh, I have plenty of reasons. Did you notice that Emily didn't argue with me? She gets it."

"I don't. I don't get it one damned bit. And I'm fucking tired of being shut out."

"Damn it. I'm not trying to shut you out." Wade's heart felt hollowed out. "It hurts to talk about it, and if you knew, you wouldn't want me." He pulled into the apartment parking lot.

"It might hurt a little less if you did talk about it. And there is nothing that could make me not want you. Hell, Wade. We're supposed to be in a damn relationship. In my universe, lovers talk to each other." Owen got out of the truck and slammed the door.

Wade whipped out of the parking lot. He could pick up his duffel later. All he wanted to do was go home and wait for the inevitable phone call from Jason. Wade had hurt Emily and he knew Jason would call him on it.

Sweat beaded on his upper lip and dread curled up in his stomach. Jason and Emily knew. Would they keep his secret?

***

Wade sealed the carton of *moo goo gai pan* and put the leftover fried rice in a plastic bag. He'd picked up a Chinese takeout meal for six, hoping it would last three or four nights. The last two demanding weeks of rehearsals began tomorrow. He would barely have time to go home and shower before reporting to the theater, and there would be at least one evening he would have to come straight from work, construction dust and all.

He was packing the last of the extra Chinese in the refrigerator when his doorbell rang. Hope flared in his chest. He'd not heard from his lover since he'd slammed out of the truck yesterday morning. But then Wade hadn't reached out either. If he did, Owen would expect an explanation Wade couldn't bear to give him.

Wade looked out the peephole. Fuck. Jason. He threw open the door and Jason stalked in. His friend went into the family room and threw himself down on the sofa. "Make yourself a home," Wade said dryly. "Would a beer help?"

"Probably not. But I'll take one anyway." Wade handed Jason a beer. Jason looked tired. "I didn't sleep much last night."

"Neither did I." Wade sat across from Jason. "Not only did I hurt Emily, I pissed Owen off big-time."

"Ouch. I take it the boy-toy doesn't like being your dirty little secret."

"Don't call him that," Wade snapped. "He's not a boy or a toy or my dirty little secret. He's a whole lot more than that."

"Sorry." Jason threw up his hands. "So what is he?"

"We're trying to have a relationship. It's been rocky."

"Been there. Done that." Jason smiled as much as his scars would let him.

"It ended well for the two of you. We may not be so lucky. Look, you didn't come over here to discuss my relationship with Owen. I hurt Emily and I'm as sorry about that. But I didn't see how I could be honest with her and not have word get back to Mom."

"Us. You hurt us. Not only Emily."

"I know, and I'm sorry."

Jason took a deep pull on his beer. "What's the big secret? Why are you so worried that it will get back to Angie? Emily said you acted like it was something terrible that had to be hidden at all costs. I don't get it. It's not the dark ages anymore. Nobody would give a damn."

"Then why did Benny break my nose and throw me out of the apartment? I came back from the emergency room and all my stuff was in a heap on the front porch. I had to go to a damn roach motel that night."

"Benny's an ass and always was."

"Benny's like everybody else in Heaven's Point and Verde. They don't cotton to queers. They wear boots and drink beer and listen to Merle Haggard."

"So do you."

Wade shrugged. "You're deliberately missing the point. The people at home are conservative with a capital C. They're not tolerant, open-minded. Russ was in the Army."

"So was I. That doesn't make us homophobes. We served beside gay soldiers and were proud to do so. Besides, with Russ's track record before he married your mom, he gave away his card to pass judgment on anybody's sex life. And you're doing the people of your hometown a serious disservice. They're good people. They might gossip a little, but they love you."

"What about Mom? She went through so much for me. How can I come out and tell her I'm no better than the rest of the Baxter family?"

"Okay. Now you really have lost me. There's no way in hell that being gay equates to what some of the Baxters are or were, and some of the abominable things they did. I agree that some of your family were real shits. You're not. And I wish to hell you'd stop believing you are." Jason leaned forward. "Angie's as good and kind as they come. The worst, the absolute worst might be a little disappointment that you won't be giving her any grandchildren. But she's got three other kids to do that. Honestly, your mother's going to love you just as much gay as she does thinking you're straight. I hope when she finds out, she's not hurt as badly as Emily was. My wife was still crying when I went to work yesterday."

"Aw, no. Damn, Jason. I didn't want to hurt Emily." Wade shook his head. "That's exactly what I don't want to happen with Mom. I don't want her to be hurt like that."

"Then tell her. Emily and I will not betray your secrets to your mother. We know how to keep our traps shut. But if you've come out, here in San Antonio, I promise you the cat's out of the bag. The word's going to make it back to Heaven's Point sooner or later. You can count on it."

***

Owen got out of his car and trudged to the back door of the Durango. He hadn't been this tired in a long time. He'd forgotten how grueling the last two weeks of rehearsals were, how much it took out of the actors and crew. It hadn't helped that the young, mostly new ensemble actors couldn't dance their way out of a paper bag. Or that Wade and Danica lacked the on-stage chemistry that had made him and Sandra so good.

They had tonight and tomorrow night to get it together. The doors opened on Friday, whether they were ready or not. Josh, Rachel, and Aubrey were all too aware of the flaws in the production, and it was making them short-tempered and snappish. A couple of ensemble players had already threatened to walk, and only a stern pep talk from Letti had kept them on board.

Owen wouldn't have minded if they'd gone. They had two left feet anyway.

Not his call. Shoving his ball cap in his waistband, he walked past the women's dressing room, currently a flurry of '60s-style dresses and hairdos, and found Wade by himself in the men's dressing room, sporting old-fashioned dress pants and a t-shirt, and holding an old-style mic and looking fed up.

"Want some help with that?" Owen asked.

"Thanks."

Wade stripped off his t-shirt and sat on a stool. Owen resisted the urge to run his hands down Wade's broad back, hooked the mic over Wade's ear, and ran the cord down the back to the box.

"Why are you using this old thing?" Owen taped the wire on Wade's neck.

"Mine's out. Doug couldn't get it to work. Josh handed me this piece of shit and told me to make do. The guys are all dressed and ready to rock, and here I am running behind."

"We'll get you caught up." Owen deftly taped the wire down Wade's back and hooked the box to the inside of Wade's pants.

Owen put on his own face mic and stashed the box in his pocket. Wade whipped his shirt on and leaned forward in the mirror.

"Your makeup looks fine."

"Thanks." Wade leaned back. "I hope it comes together better than I think it will. You missed a screaming fight between Josh and Aubrey, and, apparently, Lester and Letti had words out on the parking lot, and they're the walking pissed."

Owen rolled his eyes. "Sounds like there's more drama off the stage than on, tonight. It'll come together. It always does."

Wade smiled crookedly. "I hope so. And if not, we can console ourselves with the gang, at Thirties. You up for that?"

"I am."

A beer with Wade and the cast. He could do that.

They left the dressing room and sat in the auditorium with the assembled cast for last-minute pep talks from Aubrey and Josh. Owen glanced at Wade sitting quietly beside him. At least they weren't snapping at each other. But they weren't exactly on the best of terms either. They had endured almost a week of icy silence, broken only when they had scenes to rehearse.

They were speaking again and they'd spent one night together, but the easy camaraderie was gone. Instead, they were carefully polite. Walking on eggshells. Both loath to say anything that would destroy the fragile truce. Neither of them mentioned the buffet debacle, or said anything about Wade coming out to his family. And

Wade hadn't mentioned anything about his painful past. Whatever was eating at him, he still hadn't chosen to share it with Owen.

Which didn't bode well for their long-term chances as a couple.

Owen dragged his attention back to the pep talk. That finished, they all took their places and Jessica spent a few minutes running the ensemble through the most difficult dance scene one more time. They did a little better. Not wonderful, but they wouldn't embarrass themselves either.

The ensemble members fled to their respective dressing rooms. Owen used the restroom and was about to come out when he heard his name and "god-awful" in the same sentence. He cracked open the door, freezing when he saw the two youngest members of the ensemble standing a couple of feet away.

"I don't know why he doesn't put a paper bag over his face and be done with it," the little blonde said, her nose up in the air. "Those scars are hideous. I can barely look at him. He has no business trying to act looking like that."

The boy turned to her with exasperation. "You don't know shit, Hailey. The poor bastard got blown up defusing a bomb. It wouldn't hurt you to be a little nicer. He may be old and he may look like hell, but he's a hero."

"Whatever. I still don't think he has any business trying to act."

Owen waited until they moved away before leaving the bathroom. He pulled the hoodie up around his face and put on the baseball cap for good measure. Slinking past the actors assembling for the first scene, he took his place offstage and stood there on trembling legs, his newly gained self-confidence dissolving.

Wade and Jason were full of shit. Owens scars were too that bad. God-awful and hideous according to the girl who could barely look at him, and the boy thought he was old. The boy thought he looked like hell. They didn't think he had any business trying to act. The kids were twerps. He knew that. But twerps had a way of saying what everyone else was thinking. It made him wonder if everybody in the damn theater wished he would take his ugly face away from them.

He wouldn't do that. He would honor his commitment to *How to Succeed*. But then he'd be out of here. He'd never inflict his face on the people of the Durango again.

And he'd be damned if he'd shake hands in the lobby.

The curtain opened and he took a breath. Innate professionalism took over and he delivered a credible, if not inspired, performance. The moment the curtains closed, he jerked off his mic, made the requisite battery change, and ran out of the theater. His tires spit gravel as he peeled out of the parking lot.

His steps were heavy as he trudged up the stairs to his apartment. He flopped down on the sofa and stared into space. He'd been kidding himself. He'd honestly thought he could be part of the Durango world again. But he'd be damned if he inflicted his face on the theater people if it repulsed them so badly.

He'd rather hole up here.

And on that note, he needed a stiff drink.

He threw some ice cubes in a tumbler and was in the process of pouring a generous two fingers of whiskey when he heard a knock at the door. He considered ignoring it, but the only two people who showed up this late were Wade and Sophie.

Wade would keep banging and wake up his neighbors, and Owen didn't want to ignore Sophie. He threw open the door to a worried-looking Wade.

"Where'd you go running off to?" Wade asked. "I thought we were going to throw back a couple at Thirties."

"Fuck that. You go on to Thirties if you want to."

"I came here, didn't I? Are you going to let me in?"

"Whatever."

Wade came in and spotted the glass and the whiskey bottle. Owen looked at him defiantly and poured. He threw back the glass and gulped.

Wade's eyes bugged out. "That crap's too expensive to chug like that. You want to drink like a fish, I'll bring you some rotgut."

"I want to chug high-dollar booze, I'll chug high-dollar booze." He flopped down on the sofa and drank another generous gulp.

Wade looked at him, mystified. "What the hell is the matter?"

"Nothing. Abso-fucking-lutely nothing. Life's wonderful. All right?"

"Bullshit." Wade sat across from Owen and crossed his arms over his chest. "What's wrong?"

Something inside Owen snapped. "I'll tell you what the fuck's wrong. I'm old. I'm scarred, and I'm so damned ugly they're talking about me behind my back at the theater. I lost my career and I'm making half what I was making as a cop, and I have to rely on a disability retirement. I can't go out on that stage and sing and dance anymore. And I'm sleeping with a man who won't talk to me." He glared across the room. "You keep carrying on about thinking you're ugly because you're gay. Take a look at this mug if you think you're ugly. Shit. You're young, you're talented, and you're so damned pretty it hurts to look at you. You've got nothing to complain about. Fucking *nothing*."

CHAPTER 9

Owen's hands trembled as he downed the rest of his drink. He waited for the inevitable explosion, or for Wade to get up and walk out. That's what he would have done. But Wade sat as still as a stone and stared across at him.

"What makes you think people are talking about you behind your back?" he asked.

"I heard them. Two of the ensemble. The little blonde and her boyfriend. She said I was god-awful and hideous, and that she could barely look at me. The boy said I was old and looked like hell. Neither of them thinks I have any business trying to act. I have a mirror. I know I'm no prize to look at. But I was beginning to think maybe it wasn't so bad after all. Maybe I could get out there and do something again. If that's how people feel when they look at me, then that's a no-go."

"I see. You're going to believe a mean girl and her wimpy boyfriend?"

"Mean girls have the nerve to say what everybody else is thinking."

"I'm not so sure about that. I overheard that same snitty little blonde call Rachel a porch monkey and say Vivi Abonce was horse-faced, and that your gorgeous ex was older than dirt. I don't think I'd be too worried about her opinion."

"What?" Owen's head snapped up. "Those women are lovely."

"My point exactly. Hailey's a bitch and a troublemaker, and she can't dance worth a fuck. Josh would kick her out tomorrow if he could." Wade moved from the chair to the sofa and took Owen's hand. "People are not trash-talking you behind your back. They're not having a bit of trouble looking at you. Nobody thinks you're hideous, and they sure as hell don't think you have no business acting. They're down-on-their-knees grateful you're doing the part."

He ran his hand down the side of Owen's face. "I doubt they even see these anymore."

Wade waited for a reply. When none was forthcoming, he continued.

"Now, let's address some of the rest of what came spewing out of your mouth. I'm sorry you lost your career as a cop. No way around it, that sucks. But you like web design. Don't try to convince me otherwise. I've seen you smile and heard you humming show tunes while you work. I get that you're not getting rich. Yet. I've heard rumors that web design pays well once you build up your business." He rubbed Owen's hand. "You haven't lost the stage. You can still sing and you can still act, and I'll bet you haven't forgotten how to dance. The only thing you've lost is your nerve. You get that back, you'll be up there singing and dancing with the best of them. Knowing what that body can do, I would hardly call forty-one old."

"I wish I could believe you. About any of it. But I can't."

Wade put his arm around Owen. "Are you really gonna let one twerpy little brat set you back like this? Damn. You're still young and you're talented, and you belong on that stage. And you're so fucking sexy I can't keep my hands off you. Get it?"

"I'm trying. Honestly."

Wade took Owen by the shoulders and turned him so they were facing one another.

"You know, it would be easy for me to overwhelm you right now. To haul you to bed and fuck your brains out so you'd have to believe how young and sexy and attractive you are. But would you still believe it in the morning?" He leaned over and gave Owen the gentlest of kisses. "Or would you think I was trying to be nice?" He kissed Owen again.

"Busted." Owen's gaze was rueful. "I'd wonder."

"So what will work? What'll convince you that I find you the sexiest, most attractive, most appealing man to come my way?"

Owen felt a smile start to blossom on his face. "I'm not sure. But you could certainly try overwhelming me. That might work."

Wade's face split into a huge smile. "If you insist."

He grabbed Owen's head and yanked him over, fusing their mouths in a scorching kiss. Owen's breath caught in his throat as Wade forced his lips open, his tongue demanding entrance. Owen felt his cock start to swell as Wade bore him down into the sofa, their hands gripping one another frantically as their bodies writhed. They clung to each other for long moments, their kisses becoming more fevered. Wade's swelling cock pressed demandingly into Owen's stomach, and Wade became greedy as his hands roamed Owen's body.

Owen returned Wade's kisses and caresses with a sense of awe. There was no way Wade could fake a response like that.

They left a trail of clothes on the way to the bedroom. The next two hours were a revelation as Wade paid homage to every square inch of Owen's body with his lips, tongue, and fingers. He brought Owen to the brink enough times he thought he'd burst, each time more delicious than the last. He caressed Owen's cock with his fingers and his lips. And then they shared the ultimate intimacy, Owen crying out as spasms of pleasure rocked him from his head to his toes and Wade moaning with him. Owen then became the giver, bringing Wade to the same heights Owen had scaled.

He fell back into the pillows, replete. The assholes at the theater were wrong. He was young. He was vibrant. He was the sexiest man alive—at least in Wade's arms.

Wade turned over onto his back and drew Owen close. "Feeling better?"

"Yeah."

"Feeling on top of the world?"

"Pretty much."

"Feeling like knocking 'em dead as the book tomorrow night?"

"Yep." Owen yawned. "Sorry for the meltdown. They happen sometimes. Usually when I least expect it."

Wade tightened his arms. "Jason asked you a question the other day that you never answered. Do you ever think about the fact that you protected innocent lives on the bomb squad? That a lot of people could have been killed over the years if you hadn't done your job and done it well?"

"No, I don't. All I think about is that my partner, Robby, was a reckless fool. If he'd given me one more damn minute, I could've had it defused and it wouldn't have blown."

"Maybe you ought to think about that less, and think a little more about all the bombs you did defuse over the years."

"Wouldn't change anything."

"But it might change the way you feel about. It might make you feel a little better about your face if you could remember you got it being a hero."

"Maybe."

Wade shifted in the bed so he could look into Owen's eyes. "Have you thought any more about going to Jason's group? He'll be looking for you."

Owen shrugged. "I'm not a sharer. Talking with a bunch of soldiers who saw all kinds of horrors. I got up and went to work, came home, and slept in a bed, had running water, could order pizza."

"But the bottom line's the same. You're dealing with the aftermath of injuries, like they are. You need the support as badly as they do. You need to go, Owen. I'll go with you if it'll make things easier."

"Only if we go out for steaks afterward."

"Steaks it is. And speaking of steak, you got any food in the fridge? I didn't have time to eat dinner."

"Are you *always* hungry?"

Owen gave Wade a smacking kiss and they wandered to the kitchen, butt naked, to feast on Dagwood sandwiches and corn chips. Back in the bedroom, Wade treated Owen to another blowjob that had him trembling from his head to his toes.

Wade curled up next to Owen and was soon sound asleep, but Owen lay awake in the dark, reveling in emotions he didn't expect. Wade hadn't been faking tonight. His passion was real and undeniable. His young lover found him sexy and attractive. Although neither of them had spoken the "L" word, the scent of it had been in the air.

Scary, but a welcome surprise.

***

Wade stood next to Owen in the predawn darkness, sipping coffee from a Thermos, and shivering in the unexpectedly cool air.

"Please explain to me again why we're standing in a line that reaches all the way to the street and freezing our asses off instead of still asleep in your nice big king-size," Owen groused. "We could buy the damned iPads online."

"But not for ninety-nine dollars." Wade's lips twitched. "Besides, it's Black Friday. We're here for the experience. We're here for the ambiance. We're here for the holiday magic. Christmas is coming."

"No, we're here to lose sleep and spend money. Besides, the Christmas hype has been here since the end of August."

"Don't Scrooge."

"According to Sophie, it starts tonight with the river parade and the official lighting of the Riverwalk. Letti's mom is taking them downtown for the parade since Letti and I are both in the show tonight." Owen squeezed Wade's hand. "It was nice of you to include the kids for dinner."

"I was happy to have the kids. Sorry it was takeout. My culinary skill with a turkey leaves a lot to be desired."

Wade had ordered a smoked turkey and the trimmings from one of the local barbecue chains.

"Don't kid yourself. The kids love smoked turkey and so do I. I'm sorry you couldn't get home for dinner with your family, though."

"Missing Verde was okay. Between the play opening tonight and Mom and Russ gearing up for Black Friday at the vineyard tomorrow, it would've been eat and run anyway."

"Your family's not coming up for the play?"

"Next weekend. Which of your kids is getting the iPad?"

"I'm getting each of them one. Who's getting the ones you're buying?"

"Melanie and Jodi. Oscar already has one as well as his own laptop for school. I was surprised when he told me what he wanted. He wants a set of luggage, hard-sided, in yellow. I've already been online looking for something."

"Why yellow?"

"He thinks they would be harder to steal." Wade sighed. "He's like that about everything."

"You can take the boy out of a shitty neighborhood, but you can't take the shitty neighborhood out of the boy."

The doors to the big box store opened and the crowd surged forward. It didn't take them long to zero in on the iPads they wanted. The store was hot and Wade smiled when Owen stuffed his baseball cap in his waistband and tied the hoodie around his waist. His lover must be feeling confident again.

Owen's freak-out earlier in the week had been a reminder that he still had a long way to go in overcoming his insecurities, in reaching out and living life to the fullest. Wade knew it took time. Jason had been struggling for ten years, and it was only his love for Emily that finally inspired him to embrace life fully.

Owen had suffered the double whammy of the injuries and all they cost him, as well as coping with an acrimonious divorce from a woman he loved, but couldn't be with. He needed the same kind of motivation Emily had given Jason.

Wade looked over at his lover and sighed. Would that he could be that kind of inspiration. But he had as many issues as Owen did. He wondered how he could be Owen's inspiration when he was more fucked-up by a long shot.

They bought the last four of the advertised iPads and looked longingly at the latest wall-mount television that neither of them needed. The sun was barely peeking over the horizon when they pulled into Wade's driveway.

"Are you going shopping later when the mall opens?" Wade asked.

"Are you kidding? I'd rather stick pins in my one remaining eye than brave those crowds."

"Smart man."

"I'd rather crawl up in your bed and take a nap. Dead week took a lot out of me. It's been five years since my last one. I'd forgotten how exhausting all that rehearsing is."

"I hear you. It's been three months since my last one and I'd forgotten too."

Wade looped his arm around Owen's shoulders as they walked toward the front door. Wade's bed beckoned and they stripped down to their underwear and collapsed side by side, too tired for more than a couple of kisses before they were both sound asleep.

It was after one before either of them stirred. They feasted on leftover turkey and potato salad. A low-level buzz started building deep in Wade's gut, a buzz that would increase as the afternoon progressed and opening night grew nearer. It was always like this before the first performance. The fatigue, the doubts, even the stage fright all faded as the opening curtain grew closer. Wade tried to settle in for a few minutes of reading and then do a bit of online shopping, but it was hopeless. The play was front and center in his mind, and would be until the curtain opened and J. Pierrepont Finch came to life. He got up and paced the family room with a smile on his face.

Owen looked up from his laptop with a knowing smile. "Opening night jitters?"

"Jitters? Nah. I'm looking forward to it." He smiled at Owen. "Stupid, I know. I've had I don't know how many of these opening nights now, and I get as excited as I was the first time."

"Which is why you keep doing them." Owen stood and embraced Wade.

He could feel Owen's heart thudding against his chest.

"I love opening night as much as you do. But I don't wear a hole in the carpet."

They gave themselves plenty of extra time to fight the Black Friday traffic and arrived as Josh unlocked the back door.

He too was smiling with anticipation. "Ready to knock 'em dead?"

"Absolutely," they said in unison.

The vibe was tangible as the crew readied the stage and the cast readied themselves. Then the curtain opened, and once again Wade was swept into his character's life. Tonight, he was all about the savvy, self-confident window washer, using the advice of a book to climb the ladder of success. To his relief and surprise, Danica became the embodiment of Rosemary Pilkington. Letti stole scene after scene as Hedi LaRue. But the real delight of the evening was his scenes with "the book." Owen brought the perfect touch of tongue-in-cheek to the lines, delivering them with deadpan humor while providing a façade of gravitas to the ridiculous advice. The audience clapped and howled, and stomped their feet.

When he came out to take his bows, Owen got a standing ovation.

They took their places in the lobby and greeted their appreciative fans.

"Fantastic job, guys," Josh gushed. "The audience loved it."

"Any heavy hitters tonight?" Owen asked.

"No. But we got a call from Mr. Navarro's secretary. The Navarro Corporation bought out the entire left half of the auditorium for a week from Saturday. She told Maggie the entire San Antonio management team was looking forward to it."

Wade felt a definite twinge in the pit of his stomach. "The whole management team? Can you spell pressure?"

"Nah. If tonight's anything to go by, they'll be blown away. I promise you."

Wade sure hoped so.

CHAPTER 10

Owen pulled into the customer parking lot of the car dealership. The lights were on and he could see people moving around the showroom, looking over the new cars. He didn't see Wade's truck, but he was a few minutes early and Wade had texted earlier in the day promising to be here this evening.

Owen wandered into the showroom and was immediately approached by a young and eager salesman who encouraged him to look around for a few minutes before meeting with the support group in the conference room. He was happy to oblige, but when he saw Wade he motioned him over and together they made their way through a confusing warren of corridors and offices to a large, comfortable room in the back.

Several men and a lone woman sat talking among themselves at the large conference table where an urn of coffee, a cooler of bottled waters, and a tray of cookies awaited. A couple of the men were visibly scarred. One had a prosthetic arm. The woman had no visible scars, but the big service dog sitting beside her told a story.

Owen got a cup of coffee and sat beside Wade. The table fell silent.

Owen took a breath. "I'm Owen Aldrete. Jason invited me to join you tonight. Hope that's okay."

Sure. Absolutely. Glad to have you.

A couple more men walked in, one of them on a prosthetic leg, and then a young man in a motorized wheelchair maneuvered his way into the room.

Sheesh. And I think I have problems.

Jason came in the door five minutes later, his top button open and his tie loose around his neck. He spotted Owen and his face split into as big a smile as he could manage.

"Thanks for coming. How was opening night?"

"My man here got a standing ovation," Wade stated proudly.

"So did you," Owen added.

"Guys, Hillary, I'd like you to meet Owen Aldrete. I see he brought his best bud, and my old college roommate, Wade, with him tonight. I'm glad you're here."

Jason took control of the meeting. The people introduced themselves and shared a bit about how they came to be in the group. As they went around the table, Owen felt more and more humble, as in a sentence or two the veterans shared their stories. When it was his turn, he briefly shared the debacle that had injured him.

"I feel like a fraud sitting here with you folks. You're all heroes. I'm anything but."

The young man in the wheelchair spoke up. "Were you on the bomb squad seven years ago?"

Owen nodded.

"Then you were part of the team that defused the bomb left in the bathroom out at the county hospital. My sister works there. She said the whole east wing would have blown if it hadn't been for you. You got nothing to apologize for, dude."

The group nodded their assent. Jason threw the floor open for discussion. They talked about everything from what to do about a bleeding stump to Hillary's need to replace her aging PTSD dog. Many of the issues addressed had to do with the same self-confidence deficiency Owen was dealing with. The meeting was a revelation. He'd had no idea that wounded warriors still struggled ten or fifteen years after the fact.

But he could also see the kind of progress they'd made. They had good jobs. For the most part, they were in solid relationships. In the same way Emily had inspired Jason, something or someone had inspired them to reach out and live life to the fullest. He glanced over at Wade, who had listened attentively to every word.

The meeting lasted for the better part of an hour, and most stayed to chat after that. It was late before the last of the wounded warriors drifted out, leaving Owen and Wade with Jason.

Jason unplugged the urn and packed up the uneaten cookies. "I'll leave these in the lunchroom."

"Better here than home. That's the last thing Emily needs. Her blood sugar under control these days?" Wade asked.

"She's got a pump now. It makes all the difference. But we've been told, no more pregnancies. Riley's the last one, unless we're willing to adopt. Emily's a little disappointed. She would have loved a houseful."

"You already have a houseful," Wade remarked. "Refereed any more pee fights?"

Jason snickered and Owen laughed out loud.

"But seriously, if you and Emily want more children, the Riley family has a long history of loving adoptees. Just sayin'."

Jason nodded. "I hear you loud and clear."

"So, when are you going to come see *How to Succeed?*" Owen asked.

"We're looking at a Sunday matinee. Either this Sunday or next. When are Russ and Angie coming?"

"They're supposed to come this Friday." Wade tensed.

"Are they bringing the kids?" Jason asked.

"They always do."

"And they'll be staying the night?"

Wade nodded.

Jason looked Wade in the eye. "It would be a good time to talk to them. You'd be on your turf, not theirs. You'd also have the advantage of being able to introduce Owen. You wouldn't be in Heaven's Point with all those old ghosts haunting the discussion."

Apparently, Jason knew things Wade hadn't chosen to share with him.

"I don't know. I get what you said about Mom and Russ being good people. And you're right about Russ having no room to pass judgment. He was a dawg. But it's not only them. I have three young, impressionable siblings to consider."

Jason rolled his eyes. "After what those kids saw before they were adopted, they're not going to blink twice. Plus, there's nothing to consider. You're you, living your life, being responsible and decent. You gotta stop thinking like that."

"Yeah, then what about Gran and Gramps? They're as respectable as they come." Jason took one look at Wade and bust out laughing.

"What's so damned funny about that? Gramps and Gran are the picture of refined respectability."

Jason shook his head. "Wade, Wade, Wade. Either you're absolutely clueless when it comes to the Riley dirty linen, or your math's not worth shit. Think a minute. How old is Russ? When was he born?"

Wade quoted a date.

"Now when was his half-sister, Holly, born?"

Wade thought for a minute and his eyes grew wide. "Holy shit. Gramps had two women pregnant at the *same time*."

"Give the boy a cigar. And your Gran? She was the other woman."

A stunned Wade collapsed in a chair. "How come you know this and I don't?"

"I did the math. Emily and I had quite a laugh about it." Jason's face sobered. "Wade, the only reason I brought up your grandparents' colorful past was to make the point that none of the Rileys are in a position to judge. None of us have a say in how you live your life. None of your family is going to think less of you or love you any less. And those three siblings of yours will be fine with it. Owen's kids are okay with him, aren't they?" He sat beside Wade and put his hand on his arm. "We're not all like Benny. Got that?"

Wade nodded stiffly.

"Now, I want you to promise me, and promise Owen that you'll talk to your mom and Russ when they come this weekend. Introduce them to Owen. They're gonna like him. He's a lot prettier than I am."

That got a laugh out of Wade. He looked up at Owen and grinned crookedly. "That's what we call a hard close."

"Promise?" Jason persisted.

"Yeah. I promise."

Jason stood and hauled Wade to his feet. "Let's get out of here. It's late." He turned to Owen. "Will we see you again?"

Owen nodded. "Absolutely. Thanks for thinking to include me."

They walked out to the deserted parking lot. "Your place or mine?" Owen asked quietly.

"Yours is fine. I have a packed duffel. Condoms and lube?"

"Yeah. And before you ask, there's food too." He rolled his eyes. "You're worse than a teenager."

"I'm a growing boy." Wade laughed. They pulled up in the parking lot of Owen's apartment complex and parked side by side.

Owen let them in. "Food or sex first?"

"Food." Wade headed for the kitchen.

"Well, the honeymoon's over," Owen teased.

"Sorry about that." Wade's grin faded. "Actually, my stomach's been bothering me all day. I thought if I could get some food, it might settle down."

"Fair enough."

Thoroughly sick of turkey sandwiches, they went for a late-night supper of eggs and bacon. They polished that off and put their dishes in the dishwasher. "You feel any better?" Owen asked.

"It helped." Wade hooked his arm around Owen and pulled him close. "So would a kiss. He pulled Owen close and lowered his lips.

Owen didn't have to be asked twice. He met Wade's lips eagerly in a kiss that was warm, comforting, and sexy. As their kiss grew more fevered, Owen's hands roamed down Wade's powerfully muscled back and came to rest on his gorgeous butt. Wade held Owen in a powerful grip, plastering their bodies together from head to knees. Owen could feel Wade's erection swelling against his stomach, and he reveled in holding Wade close, kissing and touching him with abandon.

The kiss grew more passionate, and Wade grabbed him by the hand and they took it to the bedroom. Wade's clothing joined Owen's on the floor and they collapsed on the bed, a jumble of arms and legs as they indulged in a sensual tussle for top. Finally, Wade rolled on his back, letting Owen to ride him as they ground their bodies together.

"You are so beautiful," Wade murmured as he stroked Owen's face.

"You're the beautiful one," Owen rasped.

He lowered his head and kissed his way down Wade's body. He nuzzled the soft skin around Wade's navel, then continued down to surround Wade's long, wide cock. His mouth and tongue worked Wade until he was gasping.

"Let it go, babe," he urged, softly.

His lips coaxed and teased as Wade stiffened beneath him. One deep suck and Wade erupted in Owen's mouth, thrusting up as jets shot down Owen's throat. Owen tongued Wade's cock until the last tremor. Then he looked up and grinned at his cowboy

"Cocky much?" He sat up and pushed Owen into the sheets. "My turn."

Owen lay back and looped his arms around Wade. He began moaning as Wade worked magic, each caress the best kind of torture. By the time Wade took Owen's cock into his mouth, Owen was trembling, and close to blowing. It didn't take long before he erupted with a strangled shout.

Wade's lips continued to work their magic until the last tremor faded. Owen reached out and caressed Wade's shoulder. "You love me," he said in wonder. "You'd have to love me to touch me like that."

Wade lay facing Owen. "You love me too. I've never had a man make me feel the way you do." He kissed Owen lightly.

He draped his arm over Wade's side. "You're the first man I've ever fallen in love with."

Wade's eyes widened. "Really?"

Owen laughed. "Why is that so surprising?"

"You've been out awhile, and probably had your share of boyfriends. You didn't love any of them?"

"Nope. You?"

Wade shook his head. "I never let any of them get close enough. You broke through a hell of a lot of barriers." He smiled. "And I guess Friday night, you'll break through one more."

Owen sat up. "You meant it. You weren't blowing smoke up Jason's ass."

"I couldn't get away with that if I wanted to. They're family, remember?"

"If the rest of the family is as nice as they are, I'm looking forward to meeting them. How do you want to do this? You talk to them Friday night and I meet them Saturday?"

Wade thought a minute. "Or I could introduce you Friday night in the lobby after the show. That way they'll already have met you when I talk to them later that evening. That might help them some with accepting, if they've already seen how nice you are."

"Or they'll have it figured out by the time they get home," Owen said dryly.

"Well, there's that. I really would like to introduce you first. If they're okay with it." Owen nodded.

"We can go out for lunch on Saturday before they go home."

"Sounds like a plan."

Wade winced. "Damn. It hurts."

"Stomach still bothering you?"

"Probably stress. Coming out to Mom on Friday, putting on the best show ever for the Navarro contingent on Saturday. An ordinary weekend in the life of Wade Baxter."

Owen kissed him gently. "It'll all be fine. I promise."

Wade nodded and closed his eyes.

Owen pulled him close and hoped he could make good on the promise he'd made.

***

Wade stepped out of the shower and grabbed a towel. His stomach was tied up in knots and had been since last night. Damn, he hadn't had an attack of nerves this bad in years. Five to be exact, when on the hot August afternoon his mother had nearly died taking a bullet meant for him.

He'd thrown up repeatedly that evening, wearing a path in the linoleum from the hospital waiting room to the adjoining restroom. But that had been a reaction to something that had already taken place. Tonight, his anxiety was about what was going to happen. He was going to introduce the man he loved to the family he held dear. And he was going to have to deal with whatever fallout that caused so tomorrow night he could put on a performance worthy of the generous contribution from the Navarros. If that wasn't enough pressure to give him a stomachache, he didn't know what was.

He pulled on jeans, a tee, and his boots. For the hundredth time, he regretted letting Jason talk him into this. He should have taken one look at the determined car salesman and run for the hills. But a promise was a promise. He would tell his mother the truth. And hope to hell his honesty didn't destroy everything she felt for him.

He was almost to the door when a wave of nausea hit him with the force of a tsunami. He staggered to the bathroom and the ham sandwich and iced tea he'd gagged down before the shower spewed into the toilet, followed by the remains of his lunch and a mid-afternoon cinnamon roll.

He ran a finger down his throat to make sure his stomach was empty, and when he finished with the dry heaves, he rinsed his mouth and changed his sweaty tee. Taking deep breaths, he sat on the bed until the worst of the nausea subsided, and then he headed for the theater praying the nausea, stomach cramps, and nerves wouldn't affect tonight's performance.

The Verde Vineyard crossover was already in the theater parking lot, sitting a few parking places down from a brand-new pickup truck with mud on its fenders. He parked and started toward the crossover when the driver's side and passenger doors of the pickup opened and the occupants emerged, one of them stumbling a bit. *Shit, shit, shit.* Wade took a ragged breath and stared in horror across the parking lot. Pain lanced through his stomach and a wave of nausea had him gagging. Of all nights for those two to show up. His worst nightmare had come to life.

His uncles had decided to join the party.

His narrow-minded, racist, homophobic uncles were here in the flesh.

Wade froze midstride. He wondered what in God's name had prompted them to come. They'd attended only one performance, a couple years ago when he and Sandra had acted opposite one another in *Kiss me, Kate.* And they hadn't been impressed.

"Bunch of faggots singing and dancing, if you ask me," Abel had announced in the lobby. "I'd much rather see a Chuck Norris movie any day."

Denton had said nothing. But the disdain on his face had spoken volumes.

Fuckin' hell. The thought of introducing Owen to Russ and his mom had been unnerving enough. He hadn't factored in what Denton and Abel would think. Or what would come out of their mouths. He felt sweat break out on his forehead. He'd geared himself up to coming out to the Riley family. There was a pretty good chance they'd be okay with it.

But the Baxter brothers? No. Way. In. Hell.

Wade's hands shook. There was no way he would be introducing Owen tonight. It would have to wait. Owen was going to be furious. He wouldn't understand. He would think Wade was wimping out and reneging on a promise. Maybe he was. But there was no way he was exposing himself, his lover, or his mother to Denton and Abel's contempt. Because the contempt wouldn't stop with him and Owen. His mom would never hear the end of it from his uncles, for raising a Baxter to be a queer.

He wished he could get back in the truck and sleep until he woke up from this nightmare. But Russ and his mother and the kids were piling out of the crossover, all dressed for an evening at the theater.

He loped across the lot and gave them all a big hug. "What's with the uncles?" he whispered to his mother.

"They invited themselves," she whispered back. "Abel's drunk as a skunk. We'll try to keep him under control."

"Not sure what you did to deserve them showing up, but I wish you hadn't done it," Oscar added, earning himself a dirty look from his mother.

Wade turned as his uncles approached them and forced himself to smile.

"Thanks for coming," he said as he held out his hand.

Denton shook hands solemnly and nodded. His relationship with his older uncle had been strained since the debacle five years ago, but Denton had tried to be decent, paying the last semester of Wade's college tuition out of his modest salary as a deputy sheriff when his mother had been unable to. Wade turned to Abel. The smell of alcohol on his breath almost had him gagging.

Abel was an ass and a drunk. Wade hadn't been surprised when the SOB lost his teaching job two years ago for coming on to one of his senior girls. Abel was now scraping by out on the old Baxter homestead, drinking himself into a stupor every afternoon. Out of respect for Denton, Wade tried to be cordial to Abel.

Abel grabbed his hand and pumped it up and down. "Denton wanted to come. I hope this show's not as faggy as the last one. Is that pretty piece of ass you live with in this one, too?"

Oscar rolled his eyes. "I told you, Abel. She moved out awhile back. Wade's a bachelor again."

"Wow. Free to chase the ass the city girls give away these days. Damn, I bet you have some fun in this town."

If you only knew. "I've got to get in there and get ready. Does everyone have a ticket?"

"Taken care of," Russ assured him. He leaned into Wade. "I'll try to keep him from embarrassing you too badly in there tonight."

"Thanks." Wade fled across the parking lot and into the theater.

He made it to the restroom in time to throw up again. Damn it. And he hadn't even talked to Owen yet. He hoped to hell Owen understood. But he didn't really expect him to.

Wade was putting the finishing touches on his stage makeup when Owen came bouncing in the dressing room. His eyes were bright, and he had a big smile on his face. He was dressed a bit better than the jeans and tee he usually wore, sporting a button-down shirt and khaki slacks. Wade's mood dropped even more. Owen had gone all out for an introduction that wasn't going to happen.

"Are you ready to introduce me to your mama?" he whispered into Wade's ear.

"It's not going to happen tonight." Wade's lips were stiff as he applied the last of the cheek color.

Owen's smile disappeared and his eyes blazed. "What the hell? You promised. Why'd you turn chickenshit again?" Anger and hurt colored his face.

Wade clenched his jaws and fought down another wave of nausea. "I'm sorry. I'm not trying to hurt you. I'll explain after the show."

"You're damn right you'll explain," Owen snarled, then backed away. "You know what? Never mind. There is no explanation."

"There is. And I'll be happy to share it after the show. Now either help me with this damn mic or get out of the way so somebody else can."

Owen grabbed his own mic and stomped out of the dressing room.

Guess he's not going to help.

Wade handed his mic box to Lester. "Can you help me with this thing? Curtain's in fifteen minutes and I feel like hell."

CHAPTER 11

He was going to give that chickenshit son of a bitch a piece of his mind.

Owen stood in the wings, waiting to come out and take his bows. He wondered if he would get a standing ovation, or if anybody would even clap for him. His performance had been off. As had Wade's. That spark, that something that had made them so great together last weekend was nowhere to be found this evening. They had done all right. They were both too professional to do otherwise. But all right and professional wasn't going to cut it tomorrow night in front of their biggest benefactor. He and Wade would have to come to some kind of understanding about their relationship between now and tomorrow night's performance. Or they were going to blow it in front of the Navarros, and those big checks that made Josh and Cameron so happy would disappear.

But Owen had no idea what kind of consensus they would be able to reach. His hands had trembled throughout the entire performance, hurt and anger warring as he thought about Wade's last-minute brushoff. He was tired of Wade's fear and secrecy. He was tired of being Wade's dirty little secret. He'd had enough.

If Wade wasn't willing to acknowledge him to the Riley family, Owen wasn't sure he was willing to stick around. The mere thought of breaking it off lanced through him like a sword. But better a quick, sharp amputation than a slow, corrosive poisoning that ate him up over time.

Much to his surprise, he got a standing ovation. He trooped up the aisle with the rest of the cast and lined up with them in the lobby. Rather than take his usual place at the end of the line, by the lobby Christmas tree, he slipped in beside Lester and Letti. With only a couple cast members between Lester and Wade, he would be able to tell when Wade's family came through. He could watch them interact with Wade and might get something of an idea as to why Wade was so unwilling to be honest with them.

Letti looked over at him with her usual snark. "Spying on lover boy tonight? I saw his mother earlier. And the gossip mill has it you two had words in the dressing room."

"That's exactly what I'm doing," Owen said curtly. "And I'd appreciate it if you kept your sarcastic cracks to yourself."

"Whatever."

They were about halfway through shaking hands when he heard a loud booming voice over the crowd. Letti looked over toward Wade and groaned. "Oh, shit. Poor Wade. I wonder what that asshole's gonna do to embarrass him tonight."

Owen glanced over to his cowboy. He recognized the mother and her husband from Wade's pictures, but his gaze was drawn to the two tall, middle-aged men standing beside them. One of them was the living image of Wade in thirty years. His father, maybe? The other looked enough like him that he must be related. Wade had never mentioned his father or said anything about his father's family except to say the Baxters were "ugly."

Owen leaned over to Letti. "Is one of them his father?"

"Uncles. I have no idea about his father."

So Wade hadn't been forthcoming with anyone about his family.

The uncles, one of them weaving on his feet, shook Wade's hand. "Good job, boy," the inebriated one boomed. "Not sure why you want to sing and dance with all these faggot actors, but you did a damn fine job."

The actors on either side of Wade looked horrified. Lester's lip curled and Letti's brows came together. "Asshole," she murmured under her breath.

Wade looked resigned. "Uncle Abel, I love working with the people of the Durango. These men and women are some of the most talented actors and crew in San Antonio," he said with dignity. "It's an honor to perform with them."

"Fags and Meskins. You gotta be kidding me." The man let out a belch.

Fags and Meskins? Great. He was a two-fer bigot.

The other uncle looked neither surprised nor disapproving. Owen was beginning to understand why Wade had called off the big introduction.

The younger brother Owen recognized from the picture rolled his eyes. "Abel, don't be an ass," he said. "I'm a Meskin, remember?"

"I ain't likely to forget it," Abel grumbled at the boy, and Russ urged the asshole down the line. He and the other uncle, who introduced himself as Denton, dutifully shook hands with Lester and Letti and then with Owen, and moved along. But Wade's younger brother Oscar, who looked familiar, held Owen's hand for a moment and looked at him critically.

"I know you from somewhere."

"I know you, too," Owen said. "But I can't place where."

The blonde sister, Melanie, looked up at Owen. "Are you a deputy?" she asked slowly.

"I used to be a policeman." He looked again at the three children and it snapped. "Trailer park. Austin Highway."

"I remember now," Oscar said slowly. "You were one of the cops who came that night. You told us our mom was dead and we had to go with the social worker." He turned to the youngest sister. "He gave you that stuffed bunny and held you on his lap while you cried."

Russ shook his hand. "So you're one of the heroes who rescued my kids. Thanks, man."

"Oh my God, thank you." Angie, Wade's mother, a beautiful woman with a deep Kentucky accent, shook his hand also. "Lord knows what would've happened to them if you hadn't found them." She looked at the three kids and then over at Wade. "My children. They are the absolute light of my life."

"Well, according to this young man, they were doing fine when we found them." Owen laughed at Oscar's embarrassment. "He wasn't amused that night." He turned to the boy. "Still mad at me?"

"Aw, hell no. Thanks for saving us." To Owen's surprise, the boy pulled him into a big hug.

Abel looked at him curiously. "So you're a cop."

"I was until I got hurt."

"Well, tell me this. How can a cop, a real-damn-life hero like you, stand working here with all these panty-waisted fags? I mean, really. Don't they give you the creeps?"

Silence pooled around them. It seemed the entire theater waited with bated breath to hear how he would reply. "Actually, sir, working with gay men and women doesn't bother me in the least. Why would it? I'm gay." He made himself smile graciously.

Abel stumbled backwards. "*You* are a *fag? Well, shit.*"

"Way to go, Uncle Asshole," Letti murmured.

Owen glanced around. Russ and Angie were beyond embarrassed. Oscar looked disgusted, and Wade looked like he could have gladly fallen through the nearest crack in the floor. And the curl of Denton's lip as he looked at Owen? Abel said what Denton was thinking.

No wonder Wade hadn't wanted any introductions tonight.

"And on that note, I believe we'll be saying 'good night,'" Russ stated.

He took Abel's arm and steered him toward the door, the rest of the Rileys following closely behind them.

"Wasn't that fun?" Letti said brightly. She turned to Owen. "Did you see what you were looking for?"

"And I thought you and I had the family dynamics from hell."

"We don't hold a candle to a lot of families." She looked over at Wade, who was looking pale beneath the stage makeup. "This is the second time that *pendejo*'s done something like that to Wade. The Baxter family must be a doozy."

Owen was beginning to agree with her.

They shook hands with the rest of the patrons. Owen changed out the batteries in his headset and headed for the car. He had the doors unlocked and was about to crawl in when he heard his name. Wade came across the parking lot, bent a little at the waist and clutching his stomach. "I wanted to tell you how sorry I am for this evening."

"You are?"

"Damn it, Owen, I told you before the show I was sorry."

Owen laid his hand on Wade's arm. "You misunderstand. You have nothing to apologize for. I don't blame you one bit for not wanting to introduce me in front of those assholes. And your uncle's behavior in the lobby…you don't have to apologize for him. What he did tonight, that's on him and only him." He threw his arm around Wade for a hug.

"But I'm sorry. It was more of the Baxter ugliness coming out." Wade sighed. "The Baxters have a lot of ugly."

"I wouldn't be too worried if a homophobic drunk's the worst of it."

Wade snorted. "The homophobic drunk's the tip of the iceberg. Believe me, Uncle Abel's nothing compared to some of the rest of the family." He leaned over and kissed Owen. "I'm sorry I couldn't introduce you tonight. Especially with your fancy duds and all."

"So am I. But I understand."

Owen watched Wade as he walked to his truck. So the drunk homophobe wasn't the worst of it. He was merely the tip of the iceberg. Owen shook his head and got in his car.

If that asswipe was the tip of the iceberg, the rest of the Baxter family must be pretty fucking bad.

***

Wade unlocked the door and Mom, Russ, and the kids trooped inside. The pain in his abdomen was a steady pulse at this point, and nausea was assaulting him in waves. His performance had been shit tonight, and everybody in the cast noticed. But between the stomach pain and his anxiety over Denton and Abel's surprise appearance, he'd barely been able to deliver his lines or carry a tune. Owen's performance had been off as well. Tonight's audience didn't seem to notice, but tomorrow night's would. He had to get his head on straight and his nerves calmed before curtain tomorrow night, or he could end up costing the theater their next big contribution.

Mom put a homemade cake on the counter. The kids went straight for the refrigerator. "There are two made-up pizzas in the fridge and a couple bagged salads. Is that all right for supper?" he asked his mother.

"As long as you include some wine. A big glass of wine."

"I want something a lot stronger than that." Russ went straight to Wade's liquor cabinet and got out a bottle of whiskey.

Mom turned to Oscar. "I'm exhausted. You okay cooking the pizza?"

Oscar rolled his eyes. "I've been cooking since I was five, Mom."

"Go for it." She kicked off her shoes.

Wade found an unopened bottle of Pinot Grigio and uncorked it for his mother. She poured a generous glass and handed Russ a whiskey tumbler. "You want anything?" she asked Wade.

"Nah, my stomach's been acting up all day. Stress. I'm afraid alcohol will make it worse."

"All day? Something going on?"

Here was his opening to tell them about Owen. But this wasn't the best time to do it. Not with the kids underfoot, cooking supper, and listening to every word. Besides, Mom and Russ were already upset by Abel's atrocious behavior this evening. He didn't want to hit them with a heavy discussion on top of it.

"Pissed off at Abel, of course. I knew there would be trouble the minute I saw him get out of the truck. My stomach hurt during the entire performance. And I'm as worried as hell about tomorrow night. The Navarros bought out the entire left side of the theater. They're our most generous benefactors and they expect the best."

"Which I'm sure you'll deliver." Russ poured a generous slug of whiskey into the tumbler. He held up the glass in a toast. "To Abel Baxter. The biggest fucking asshole in three counties." He threw back half the glass.

"Here, here." Mom polished off a third of her wine. "Damn that son of a bitch. Embarrassing you in front of your theater friends like that."

"Yeah. Dad told Denton to put his asshole brother in the truck and get him the hell back to Verde tonight, and for fuck's sake not to show their faces over here. His cuss words, not mine." Oscar's grin was wicked.

Wade collapsed onto a barstool. "Did you really expect anything different?" he asked tiredly.

"He's getting worse," Russ said. "He's always been an asshole. But before all the shit went down that summer, he could at least hold a job, and he had a little respect for some of his neighbors. Now he's an asshole to everybody, even people he used to like. And I know he's had two midafternoon DWI's. Another one and his license is toast." He took another healthy swig of whiskey. "What happened with your mom and your grandmother sent him on a downward spiral he can't seem to climb out of."

"I'm not sure why it sent him into a spiral," Mom snapped. "I was the one with the bullet hole in me. Not him."

Wade shrugged. "He's a Baxter. What do you expect?" He looked at his mother sadly. "Do you think we'll ever be free of the Baxter ugliness?"

Mom was quiet a minute. "I don't know, Wade. And you're making it sound like the Baxters are nothing but awful. Sure, there was a lot of ugliness involved with that family. But they also produced you. And, child of mine, you are anything but ugly."

His mother didn't know about him yet. Wade wondered if she would still feel that way when she found out the truth.

The thought made his stomach hurt that much worse.

He tried eating some pizza and cake with the family, but it came right back up, along with the ginger ale his mother made him drink to settle his stomach. As the night passed, the pain grew worse, to the point he was inches from screaming. *This isn't stress.* Something else was wrong with him.

He wished Owen were here.

He got up to throw up again and found his mother waiting when he got out of the bathroom. "Hell. Did I wake you up?"

"You may be a grown man, but you're still my son. I can sense things." She pushed him down on the bed and felt of his forehead. "Jesus, Wade. You're burning up. Stress wouldn't give you a fever like that."

A rumpled and unshaven Russ poked his head in the room. "Fever? Crap. Lay back." Russ pushed Wade back on the bed and stuck a finger in his abdomen on the right side. Wade buckled and let out a bellow of pain. "Yep. Appendicitis. I'd bet my December profits that's what's wrong. Get some clothes on. I foresee a trip to the emergency room in your future."

Appendicitis? Wade cursed under his breath. There was no way he could do the show tonight if he was that sick. He started to call Owen. No, he'd wait. Russ could be wrong. It could be something less serious, like food poisoning. He might be over that in time to perform.

He'd wait until he knew more before alerting the Durango.

"Give me a minute. I'm coming, too. I'll wake Oscar. He can take care of the girls until I get back." Mom took off toward the other bedroom.

Russ helped Wade into a pair of sweats and a dry tee, and found his flip-flops in the closet. Wade hobbled to the family room, every step agony. A sudden burst of even more intense pain caught him in the midsection, and he bent double and collapsed on the couch.

Sweat ran down his forehead and dripped into his eyes. He let out with a series of curses that would have done his little brother proud.

He'd never hurt so badly in his life.

Russ and his mother appeared less than five minutes later, looking remarkably well put together under the circumstances. Each of them took an arm and they half-carried him out to their car. Wade handed his mother his wallet and phone, and when he said he had no regular physician here in San Antonio she did a quick search and found the closest emergency room that would take his insurance. Ironically, it was the same emergency room Letti and Sophie were taken to after the accident.

At least Owen would know where to find him.

Russ pulled up under the portico and Mom darted inside, returning momentarily with an aide and a stretcher. The triage nurse took one look at Wade and bumped him to the head of the line. The aide whisked him into a cubicle and his nurse helped him get into a bigger gurney and a hospital gown.

The nurse got an IV started, and for the next hour and a half a parade of health care professionals wandered in and out of his cubicle. The doctor ordered a trip upstairs for a CT scan and then to a room on the med-surg floor, where they parked the bed-sized gurney and gave him something to ease the pain, which left him in a haze.

Russ went downstairs long enough to get coffee, and he and Mom fidgeted impatiently sipping their coffee and wishing out loud that things were moving more quickly.

A different doctor came in carrying a large iPad. He identified himself as the hospital's radiologist and said he had the results of Wade's scan. "Mr. Baxter, the news isn't good. The scan shows that your appendix has already burst. I have an operating room reserved for ten this morning, and a surgeon on the way." He looked at Wade. "How long have you been having symptoms?"

Wade had to think a minute. "I think it was hurting on opening night."

"Opening night? Wade, that was a week ago," Mom wailed.

"It definitely hurt Tuesday." Wade could feel himself start to fade.

The doctor looked at him and shook his head. "You should have come in sooner."

"I thought it was nerves. The play. The Navarros. Owen." He fought to keep his eyes open.

"How sick is he?" Mom demanded.

Wade blinked. *Pretty damned sick, Mom.* How sick, he didn't know. All he knew was that he wasn't going to be doing the show tonight.

The show. He needed to call Owen. Right now.

The doctor started with a river of medi-babble that went right over Wade's head, but his mother seemed to understand. The doctor left, and Wade motioned to his mother.

"I need you to call Owen. Number's in my phone."

"Owen?" She dug his phone out of her handbag. "Don't you want me to call Josh?"

"Owen Aldrete. You met him last night." Damn, he was about to go to sleep.

"The cop Oscar recognized," Russ prompted her.

"Tell him what's happened. He'll know what to do."

Wade's eyes fluttered shut and he went to sleep, confident that Owen would be there soon.

CHAPTER 12

Owen stared at the computer screen and sipped his coffee. He tried to concentrate on the half-constructed webpage in front of him, but his mind kept drifting to the scene in the lobby last night. He couldn't begin to imagine Wade's mortification at his uncle's performance. It was no wonder Wade had so many hang-ups about being gay, especially if his uncle's attitude was typical in the small town he'd grown up in. Surely everyone in the little Hill Country burg didn't feel or act like Abel Baxter. But if a lot of them did, it would be enough to make Wade think twice about being honest about himself.

Owen still believed honesty would be the best policy with his mother and her husband. They both seemed nice. But he doubted that honesty would be forthcoming any time soon. Wade said his family was headed home this afternoon and probably wouldn't be back to San Antonio until after Christmas. Which meant it would be at least a month, maybe more, before he had a chance to talk to them on his terms. Which would give him plenty of time to talk himself out of leveling with them. Owen sincerely hoped that wouldn't happen. But he wouldn't be surprised if it did.

He moved some of the components around on the website's home page and tried a new font for the headers. Nope. He returned to the original font and was about to pop another pod in the coffee machine when his phone buzzed. He looked down at the screen and smiled. *Wade.* Owen's heart lifted. Maybe brunch with the Riley family was still on. Maybe Wade had talked to them last night after all. He clicked on his phone. "Wade?"

"Is this Owen Aldrete?"

Owen recognized the voice immediately. The woman with the deep Kentucky accent could only be Angie Riley. "This is Owen Aldrete. Is everything all right, Mrs. Riley?"

"I'm afraid not. Wade's here at the Medical Center. His appendix burst last night and he's going into surgery this morning at ten. He was adamant that I call you and let you know. He said you'd know what to do."

Wade. Burst appendix. Hospital. Icy tendrils of fear wrapped themselves around him. This wasn't a simple case of appendicitis. If the appendix had already burst, Wade's system had been flooded with all kinds of microbes, none of which belonged in the human body. Owen's heart pounded in his throat. Wade was a sick man.

He had to get to the hospital.

"I'll be right there, ma'am. What room is he in?"

"Four-twelve. Should I call Josh and let him know?"

"I'll take care of that. You take care of Wade."

Owen saved the webpage and shut down the computer. He threw on jeans and a Henley that had seen better days, and sprinted to the car. Wade would be all right, he assured himself as he laid rubber getting out of the parking lot.

He couldn't begin to imagine the alternative.

He left a message for Josh and woke Rachel, who promised to find Josh and bring him to the hospital. The early morning traffic was light, and Owen made the twenty-minute drive in under fifteen.

Rather than wait for an elevator, he sprinted up the four flights of stairs and burst into the hall, making one wrong turn before coming to a halt in front of Wade's room. He paused a minute to catch his breath. He heard a couple of voices, neither of them Wade's. He pushed open the door. The privacy curtain around the bed was open. Angie Riley was standing by the bed holding her son's hand. Russ was hunched over on a worn futon frantically texting. An ashen Wade appeared to be asleep.

"How is he?" Owen demanded.

If the Rileys were surprised he'd gotten there so quickly, they didn't show it. "They gave him something to knock him out. He's been asleep since I called you," his mother said. She reached out and stroked Wade's face. "Apparently, he's been sick for a week."

Owen stepped over to the bed and looked down at Wade. "Why didn't he do something?"

Angie shrugged. "He chalked it up to stress. He said he'd been under a lot lately."

Owen gulped. Wade had blamed his stomachache on stress. Stress Owen had heaped on him. He and Jason Donahue should have kept their mouths shut. They should have left well enough alone. Instead, Wade had worried so much about coming out to his family, he hadn't realized something else was making his body hurt. Owen cursed under his breath.

He'd helped put Wade in that hospital bed.

One he wasn't going to be out of any time soon.

He reached out and took Wade's other hand and squeezed it. Wade's eyes flickered open.

"You came," he murmured sleepily.

"Of course I came."

"Thought...thought you might still be mad."

"I'm not mad."

"Don't leave," he said, clinging tightly to Owen's hand.

"I'm not going anywhere."

Wade drifted off to sleep. Owen ignored the puzzled looks on Angie and Russ's faces and held onto Wade's hand. A few minutes later an orderly came into the room. "It's time to take Mr. Baxter down to the O.R.," he told them.

Owen and Angie tried to let go of Wade's hands, but he clung even more tightly to them.

"Wade, honey, you have to go to the operating room," his mother said gently.

Wade's eyes opened a slit. "Kiss for luck, Mom."

"Kiss for luck." Angie leaned down and kissed Wade's forehead.

Wade turned to Owen. "Kiss for luck, Owen."

Uh-oh. Angie and Russ's eyes flew open and they stared at the two of them. But the plea in Wade's eyes overrode everything else. Owen leaned down, intending to kiss Wade on the forehead as Angie had done, but with a surprisingly strong arm, Wade reached up and pulled Owen's mouth down to his.

He gave Wade a tender kiss, his lips firm but gentle, lingering until he felt Wade relax. His eyes were swimming with tears when he raised his head.

"Kiss for luck. Now let this man get you downstairs so they can make you better."

He and Angie backed away. The orderly whisked Wade out of the room. Owen grabbed a paper towel and wiped his eyes, careful not to dislodge the glass one in front of the Rileys.

"I called Josh and Rachel. They'll be here in a few."

"The surgical waiting room is in the basement, close to the operating rooms," Angie said. "Thank you for calling them."

"Of course. I'll text them and let them know where to find us." Russ and Angie nodded.

She reached out and put a gentle hand on his arm. "The doctor assured us he'll be all right."

Owen nodded, too overcome to speak. Ignoring the speculation in their eyes, he backed out of the room and fled down the hall. There went introducing Owen at the theater. There went having a quiet talk with Angie and Russ. There went easing them into the truth. Wade had outted himself to his mother and stepfather in the bluntest way possible. He'd planted a big, juicy kiss on his lover's lips right in front of them.

Wade was going to be an unhappy camper when he realized what he'd done.

Owen's stomach growled. Damn. He'd run out of the apartment without breakfast. He fired off a text to Rachel telling her where the waiting room was and asking her to bring him something to eat.

The waiting room was almost empty. He'd downloaded a couple of bestsellers on his reading app, but he couldn't concentrate. Despite Angie's reassurance, he was still worried sick and would be until Wade was out of the operating room and on the road to recovery. He gave up on reading and was scrolling through his emails when Josh and Rachel appeared, carrying a big sack from a popular taco place.

"How's Wade?" Josh demanded.

"Not good."

They sat beside him and he gave them a quick rundown.

Rachel rummaged around and handed Owen a napkin and a couple of foil-wrapped tacos.

"Egg and chorizo for you. Egg and bacon for Josh and me."

"Thank you." Owen unwrapped a taco and wolfed it down in three bites.

They spent a few minutes killing most of the tacos. Angie and Russ came in and sat a few chairs over. Rachel offered them the rest.

"Thanks." Angie smiled tiredly. "We didn't get to eat this morning."

Josh wadded up the aluminum foil and tossed it into a nearby trashcan.

"We've got a problem."

Owen nodded. He'd been so worried about Wade, he really hadn't thought about the position Josh was in right now with the Navarros coming tonight and his lead actor in the O.R. "That's the drawback to community theater. There's no such thing as an understudy."

Rachel nodded. "True. But most of the time, there's somebody around who played the part in the past who can step in. I don't know what we're going to do tonight. There's nobody who's ever done the J. Pierrepont Finch role before."

"Actually, there is." Josh gave Owen a level look. "You weren't going to tell me, were you?" He turned to Rachel. "Owen's played the role. Letti told me."

"You have?" Rachel said eagerly. "Then we can—"

"Whoa. Not so damned fast." Owen looked from Josh to Rachel. "Me? Do J. Pierrepont Finch, tonight? No way in hell."

"Jesus, Owen. How can you turn us down, knowing how badly we need you up on that stage? You know what's riding on tonight." Josh ran his fingers through his hair.

"Why?" Rachel demanded. "Why are you so determined not to do it? Especially under the circumstances."

"It's because of the circumstances. You don't want me up on that stage tonight. The Navarros expect the best. Wade is the best. He's young and handsome as sin. J. Pierrepont Finch was written with actors like Wade in mind."

"You've played it, too," Rachel reminded him.

"Sure, I played it fifteen years ago when I was young and handsome as sin. I'm forty-one and look every day of it. And if that isn't enough, my face looks like the special effects from a zombie apocalypse movie." He gestured toward his scars. "These show, Josh. And not only up-close. They're visible from the back of the theater."

"What if they weren't visible?" Angie Riley was looking over at the three of them. "What if those scars didn't show?"

They turned in unison toward Wade's mother. "Uh...what?" Owen asked.

"What if those scars didn't show? Would that make a difference?"

Before they could answer her, Angie Riley walked over to them, her husband on her heels. She took Owen's chin in her hand and tilted his face up to the light, turning it this way and that. "We could do it. Get those scars covered."

Owen shook his head. "Mrs. Riley, I know you mean well. But my scars are bad. There's no way makeup's gonna make them go away."

"Oh, really?" She got out her phone and flipped through the photos. "Normally I keep my clients' before and after pictures private, but I have Cathy's permission to use hers." She handed Owen her phone. "What do you think?"

He looked down at the attractive brunette. "Nice looking woman. She knows how to do a good makeup job."

"Okay. Now here's what she looks like without the makeup job."

He looked down at the picture and sucked in a breath. Without the makeup, Cathy's face was as bad as his, if not worse, with mottled burn scars and skin grafts covering most of the right side. "Amazing," he admitted. "How do you do it?"

"Some years back, Russ's sister came to me wanting me to make a concealing makeup for one of her wounded warriors. I put it together and Cathy, Holly's warrior, was my first customer. I've improved it over the years, and I sell a lot of it. My customers are covering everything from burn scars to acne pits to the psoriasis from hell. I do both mass market and custom blends."

"Cathy credits Holly for helping lasso her husband. I think the poor bastard would have fallen for her anyway," Russ teased.

"Russ, really." Angie rolled her eyes and pulled up another photo, this one of an unassuming tube of makeup.

Owen looked down at the picture. "Angie's Magic," he murmured.

Rachel's head snapped up. "That's your makeup line? You're the Angie of Angie's Magic? Wow. I didn't know. My sisters and I use your sheer stuff. Your colors for black women are the best on the market." She turned to Josh and Owen. "Wade never told us his mom's a celebrity makeup artist, or about her concealing makeup. I wonder why?"

Angie smiled. "He's a guy and probably didn't think about it. And I'm hardly a celebrity. But I like to think I do good work." She showed the before and after pictures to Rachel and Josh. "Depending on the extent of the scarring, it's good to three or four feet before a person notices. Sometimes closer. From the stage, your scars will not be visible." She leaned forward. "You'll look like you did before you were hurt. You will look like you did the first time you played the part."

"She can't do much about the forty-one birthdays, though," Russ shot out.

Josh rolled his eyes. "Please. We're trying to talk him into it, not discourage him." He turned to Owen. "Think about it. If you didn't have the scars, would you do it tonight?"

He would do it in a heartbeat. If not for the scars, he'd say, "yes" in a New York minute.

"Let me see the pictures again."

Angie handed him the phone. He flipped a couple of times between the two pictures of Cathy. "Can you really have me looking as good as she does?"

"I can."

Owen took a deep breath. He could feel his insides start to quiver. Fear? Excitement? Anticipation? Maybe a little of all three. He could do it. If she could honestly have him looking like his old self, he could get up on that stage and be J. Pierrepont Finch. "Okay. You have yourself a window washer."

Josh gave an audible sigh of relief.

Rachel gave him a high-five. "I'll call the costume designer and have her deliver a set of costumes in your size. Forty regular?"

"Forty-two."

"God, Owen. I owe you one," Josh said. "Everybody at the Durango will owe you one. And Mrs. Riley, we will really owe you one." He turned to Owen. "I have a copy of the script in the car. You want it now?"

"Yeah, I want it now."

He had a lot to do between now and curtain.

CHAPTER 13

Owen unlocked the back door of the theater and flipped on the lights. It was two hours before the curtain went up, and he was the first one to arrive. Angie had asked him to allot plenty of time for her to get him made-up before the other actors flooded the dressing room.

"It's going to take me awhile to get the makeup applied and show you how to use the product, and I don't want to be stumbling over half-naked men while we work."

"You've been backstage before." He laughed.

"Worse than a wedding."

He made his way to the men's dressing room, hunting for light switches as he went. It was eerily silent in the empty theater, every footstep echoing off the walls. He turned on all the lights in the dressing room, wincing as he caught a glimpse of himself in the mirror, the glaring makeup lights highlighting every line, red patch and blotch on his imperfect flesh. He turned back to the mirror and peered at himself closely for the first time in a long time. Damn. If the makeup could cover this kind of devastation, it really must be good.

He sat on a raised stool and opened the script. He'd spent late morning and all afternoon reviewing J. Pierrepont's lines. He'd started in the hospital, moving to a vacant corner in the waiting room away from the Rileys and the Durango crowd drifting in one at a time.

Everyone sighed with relief when the doctor told them the surgery was successful. Angie and Russ had made it a point to ask him to join them for a moment in the recovery room, but Wade had still been out of it and the nurse said it would probably be morning before he woke up entirely.

Which would probably be merciful given the long incision running across his abdomen, the painful-looking drain coming from the wound, and the nasty discharge making Owen and Angie gag in unison.

He'd gone from there to the apartment, where to his surprise, Danica was waiting for him to go through some of the dance steps. He'd gone back to the script after that, relieved that with a couple of read-throughs J. Pierrepont's lines were coming back to him. If he had any time left after getting dressed and made-up, he'd go over the dance steps on the actual stage. But right now the makeup was the most important thing.

Rachel arrived five minutes later carrying a complete set of J. Pierrepont Finch costumes in Owen's size. Angie Riley came in carrying a large pink and black striped train case.

"That's a lot of makeup," Owen said.

"This is my emergency stash. I have a rolling case for a really big job like a wedding."

Rachel hung the costumes on a rack and disappeared.

Owen asked, "Mrs. Riley, how's Wade?"

"First off, please lose the 'Mrs. Riley.' That's Russ's mother. Besides, I'm three years younger than you. Call me Angie."

"Gotcha. Where do you want me to sit?"

"The stool's fine if you'll turn where the lights are shining right on you. Can I take before and after pictures?"

"Sure." Owen turned this way and that until she nodded. She took a head shot with her phone, and unzipped the bag and plucked out four tubes of foundation. With deft fingers that spoke of a lot of experience, she squeezed out a little of each of them and drew four lines across his right cheek.

"Hmm. You're right between Dark Beige four and Olive one. If you decide to order some, I'll make up a custom one that blends them. Or you can do it yourself. Cheaper that way."

She wiped off the tester lines and squeezed a generous dollop of her two choices on top of her hand. She used a makeup brush to blend the thick liquid. "The first generation of this was much heavier, more like a paste. I've managed to lighten it some without sacrificing its concealing properties. How'd you get hurt?"

"Trying to defuse a bomb. Oh, the eye's a fake, if that matters."

"I don't know. I've never done a fake eye. I learn something new every day. That'll be mine for today." Her eyes twinkled as she began brushing the makeup on, starting on the undamaged side of his face.

Owen raised his eyebrow. "You learned a hell of a lot more than that in one day."

Angie was quiet for a minute. "Did I?" she asked softly.

It was Owen's turn to be silent. "You already knew about him? About us?" he asked.

"About you two? No. About Wade? I didn't know for sure until this morning. But I've suspected for a long time. Mothers sometimes know things about their children even before the children do." She brushed the rest of the foundation on Owen's face and mixed some more.

"How did you know? Wade had been so convinced he was keeping it a deep, dark secret."

"Lots of things. He had his share of girlfriends in high school, but none of the relationships ever amounted to much. Once he got to college, the girlfriends were fewer and fewer, and then he quit dating altogether. He broke up with Natalie at the end of his junior year and he's not dated anyone that I know of since then.

"At first I thought it was maybe the dysfunction in the Baxter family, which is describing them kindly, but I couldn't blame his total lack of interest in women on the Baxters."

"Sandra didn't make you think twice?"

"She and Noelle had their own wing across the house from Wade's room. There was never any spark there. And he sent her back to Tennessee without batting an eyelash. If she'd been his girlfriend, there would have been hell to pay when her husband showed up." She continued brushing the makeup on his face. "Are you and my son serious?"

"I'd like us to be. It's been hard. We have issues."

"Don't we all." Angie mixed some more foundation. "Issues specific to you being gay, or the usual run of issues?"

Owen thought a minute. "Some of each. Wade thinks I should be acting. He doesn't understand why I don't want to show these scars to the world."

She smiled a little. "Well, you won't be showing them to anybody tonight." She started stroking makeup on his scarred forehead. "Ahh. This is working like a charm. You're gonna look good." She dipped the brush and painted on a little more. "And the other issues? Or is that too personal?"

"Not really. Wade's had a hard time accepting himself. I don't get it. He's got this hang-up about being gay and ugly. He says he doesn't think being gay is ugly. He assures me he doesn't find me ugly or what we do together ugly. But he persists in thinking that because he's gay, he's somehow ugly. He keeps talking about being gay, being a Baxter, and how that makes him ugly. After I'd finally convinced him they're not going to care, he finally came out to the theater crowd, but he's been scared to death of coming out to you. He says he doesn't want to expose you to any more of that family's ugliness. And he's terrified it'll change your feelings for him."

"Oh, dear sweet Jesus. My poor baby." Angie's eyes filled with tears. "Those sons of bitches. I knew it was bad. I've known for years that the things they did to him damaged him, but I didn't know how badly."

Owen handed her a tissue from the dispenser. She wiped her eyes and blew her nose. "What is that story, anyway? What did they do to him that messed with him so badly?"

"How much has he said to you?"

"Absolutely nothing other than to say the Baxters were ugly. I do know he dreams something about you and his grandmother because he keeps screaming 'no' throughout the nightmare. He had one of those the first night we were together."

"Shit. I thought those stopped years ago." She resumed stroking on the foundation. "Nothing else?"

"Nothing. So little that I thought maybe one of his uncles was his father until my ex told me differently."

"That bastard's dead." She mixed some more color and stroked it across his scarred cheek. "You're worried about these scars on your face. Honey, these are nothing compared to the scars Wade carries. But his don't show."

"Scars on the heart usually don't."

"Good. You get it. His scars are way deeper and uglier than yours, and I don't have a magic makeup to do anything about those." She continued down his cheek and onto his neck. "Damn, I'm going to have to go all the way down below your collar. Lose the shirt."

Owen pulled off the Henley, careful to hold it away from his partially made-up face. She continued down to a little below where the window washer tee shirt would come to.

"So what happened?"

"That's not my story to tell. It's Wade's. But he does need to talk to you. He needs to be completely forthcoming if your relationship's going to have a snowball's chance in hell."

"He doesn't want to. He insists it'll change the way I feel about him."

"Would it?"

"Hell, no. Does knowing he's gay make you feel any differently?"

"Hell, no. Nothing he could tell me would make a bit of difference." She backed up a couple of steps and looked him up and down. "Although, I may need to have a talk with him about sexy older men."

Owen reached out and gave her a one-armed hug. "Thanks for understanding."

"Get him to talk to you. Please." Owen nodded. Angie motioned for him to sit. "You want me to finish this off or do you want to do it yourself?"

"Be my guest."

She worked on his face for another twenty minutes, getting the foundation just right and applying the rest of a regular stage makeup job, using the time to explain to Owen how to apply the concealing foundation. She motioned for him to look at himself in the mirror. Owen took a look at himself and stared in astonishment.

He looked like he used to look.

He looked like he was supposed to look.

Owen Aldrete was back.

The Owen that sang and danced and graced the stage was back.

He turned to the left and the right, staring at himself in shock. He couldn't quite believe what he was seeing. Angie Riley had done it. She had restored his face to what it had been before the bomb wreaked its havoc.

The lines, the scores, the blotchy patches of scar tissue had all magically disappeared underneath her wonderful concealer. Even his eye looked more natural. He spent a few long moments looking at himself before turning to Angie, a disbelieving smile on his face that widened when she took a second picture of him. "I look like me. How can I thank you?"

"By singing my praises and buying a lot of makeup. You're going to need it. Wade's not going to be back here any time soon."

Josh came bounding in and skidded to a stop. "Holy crap. You look…you look wonderful."

Rachel followed. She took one look at him and squealed in delight. "Oh, my God. You look fantastic. You're gonna knock 'em dead."

Owen felt himself smile. "I hope so." He turned to Angie. "Can you stay?"

She shook her head. "I really need to get back to Wade. I'll leave these tubes with you, but they're not going to last much past a show or two. Go online and we can ship you some more Monday. After I go home, I'll mix up your special blend."

"Thank you." He squeezed her hand.

Angie started packing away her things. Josh started helping Owen put on the mic, and Rachel left the dressing room only to return in a moment with a put-out-looking Letti in tow.

"Yes, I know Owen's doing the role," Letti groused. "I don't see how with those scars, but—" She skidded to a stop and stared in amazement. "Shit. You look like you used to." She came closer and studied his face carefully. "Unbelievable. But you might want to put your shirt on. That's what got you in trouble in the first place." She took another look and headed out.

Owen and Josh looked at one another and burst out laughing. "My ex," he explained to a baffled-looking Angie.

Josh shook his head. "There is no pleasing her, you know?"

"I know." Owen laughed even harder.

Josh got the mic taped down his back and hooked to the inside of his briefs. Angie sailed out, and one by one the men of the cast drifted in, oohing and aahing over his transformation. He finished getting into the first costume, a window washer's overalls. The blood rushed to his ears and excitement mingled with out-and-out terror. He was going to do it. For the first time in five long years, he was going to step out on a stage in front of a live audience. He was going to sing. And dance. And bring J. Pierrepont Finch to life.

He hoped to hell he could pull it off.

A thought struck him as he stood waiting in the wings. If he was going to play J. Pierrepont Finch, who was going to voice the book? His question was answered five minutes later when Vivienne Abonce, of all people, came to stand beside him wearing a head mic and holding a copy of the script. "You?" he asked. "You're the book?"

"Rachel's idea. She thought as deep as your voice is, another deep voice would confuse the audience."

Owen nodded. Vivienne's contralto would be the perfect foil for his deep tones. "Brilliant thinking on Rachel's part."

Vivi leaned over with a wicked smile. "I'm no Wade, but maybe we can come up with some chemistry anyway." She winked impishly.

Owen grinned. "We will."

The crew chief called five minutes, and everyone quieted. He could hear Josh doing his usual pre-performance spiel. "Tonight we have a change in the program and a special treat. Wade Baxter, who was scheduled to play our lead, was taken ill this morning and is unable to perform this evening. In his place, Owen Aldrete is reprising the role of J. Pierrepont Finch. Let's give it up for Owen."

The crowd clapped enthusiastically. Owen's heart pounded in his chest. *This is it*. His hands started to tremble. Vivienne put her hand on his arm.

"Relax. You're gonna be fantastic."

He took his place on the stage. As the minutes counted down, he channeled his character. And by the time the curtain swept open, J. Pierrepont Finch was ready to come to life.

From the first scene, Owen poured everything into J. Pierrepont Finch. He acted bright, ambitious, sneaky, funny, and smart. He delivered J. Pierrepont in all his flawed but brilliant glory. He had the audience right where he wanted them, rooting for the window washer to make it to the top. He reached out to the audience, as he'd always done, giving them a character they could love. And he wasn't the only one on fire. Danica, Lester, Letti, and the entire cast was at their absolute best as they brought their characters to life. Even Vivienne, who'd had only since two this afternoon to prepare, delivered her dialogue spot-on.

Applause thundered through the theater. The crowd was on its feet before the ensemble even came out for their bows. The applause grew louder as the supporting cast appeared, Lester and Letti and Danica. But when he appeared, the entire auditorium erupted in whistles and stomps and cheers.

Owen took his bows, letting himself bask for a moment in the glory, exultant yet humble. He hadn't done it by himself. Wade, Angie, Josh, and Rachel had all been a big part of what he'd accomplished tonight.

The audience finally quieted down. The cast trooped up the aisle and lined up to greet the audience. Owen found himself standing next to Letti again. The lobby was more crowded than usual, with a sellout crowd and the Navarro management eager to meet the cast.

And eager to sing Owen's praises, as patron after patron told him how much they'd enjoyed his performance. They were about halfway through shaking hands when Josh and a woman named Maggie came down the line with an elegant couple in their sixties. Josh was introducing them personally to each cast member. "Mr. Navarro, I'd like to introduce you to Owen Aldrete. He normally plays the book voice, but kindly stepped in as our lead when Wade landed in the hospital this morning. Owen, this is Mr. and Mrs. Navarro."

So this was El Jefe. *The generous benefactor they so desperately wanted to please.*

"Glad to meet you," Owen murmured.

"You did a wonderful job," Mrs. Navarro gushed. "You made the character so much fun."

Mr. Navarro cocked his head. "Where do I know your voice from?"

Owen smiled. *"Feed me."*

The Navarros laughed. "Of course. I wanted to meet you that night. So do you normally play off-stage roles?" Mr. Navarro asked.

"Mostly," he said slowly. He wasn't about to admit it had been five years since he'd been on stage.

"Well, don't. With your looks and your talent, you're wasted back there." He turned to Josh and Maggie. "I'd like to see more of this one front and center."

Josh's eyes were dancing. "I can guarantee it, sir."

They moved on as Owen stared after them. "They didn't notice," he breathed. "They didn't look twice at my face."

"Nobody has. Except the few who know you have scars." Letti reached out and gave his hand a squeeze. "Welcome back, Owen. The Durango has missed you."

CHAPTER 14

God, what was the matter with him? He'd never been this sore in his entire life.

Wade's eyes flickered open and he looked around. He was in a hospital room. The blinds were drawn, but pink light filtered through. Morning. The curtain around his cubicle was open and someone, Russ probably, was snoring softly. He picked up his left hand and found it tethered to an IV. He had wires attached also, some to the beeping monitor in the corner. He ran his right hand down his body to where it hurt so badly and found a huge bandage with a tube coming out of it. From the way his cock felt, he had another tube jammed halfway to his kidneys.

He wouldn't be jumping Owen any time soon.

Owen. Oh, my God. Oh, *hell.* Had he really laid a kiss on Owen in front of his mother and Russ? Or had he dreamed the whole thing?

Wade took a deep breath as he struggled to remember the last few days. He had talked to Jason and was going to introduce Owen to his family. His stomach hurt all day Thursday and Friday. His uncles had shown up. He and Owen fought. His stomach had gotten worse and his mother and Russ brought him in. The doctor told them his appendix had burst. Owen had come. His mother had given him a kiss for luck. Owen had given him a kiss for luck...

Wade shut his eyes as mortification washed over him. He'd kissed Owen right in front of his mother and Russ. And it hadn't been a friendly peck on the cheek. It had been a full-out kiss on the lips. And they hadn't been shy about it. Owen had kissed him until he'd calmed enough for the orderly to take him away.

He guessed he wouldn't need to have a talk with them after all. And he sure as hell wouldn't need to introduce Owen. Now his mother knew why there had been no girls in his life for the longest time. And why he'd wished Sandra good luck so easily.

He lay quietly, trying to avoid movement, which made the pain worse. A few minutes later a bright-eyed nurse with corkscrew curls ringing her ebony face bounced in the room. "Mr. Baxter. You're finally awake. You slept away all of yesterday and through the night. On a scale from one to ten, how's your pain level?"

"Shitty," he managed to mumble. "Seven, maybe."

"I'm not surprised. With a burst appendix, they had to open you up completely to clean out the infection. Your incision is about six inches across."

"I feel every inch of it."

"This will help." She injected a dose of something into his IV. "It may take a few minutes."

He heard Russ stirring on the futon.

"Oh, good," he said. "You're awake. I finally got your mother to go home at midnight."

"Mom was here all that time?" Wade turned his head.

Russ's hair was too short to be mussed, but two days without a shave showed.

"Most of it. Once you were in recovery, she went to that boutique that carries her makeup and then to the theater long enough to make-up Owen's face. He stepped in and played your part last night."

"He did?"

"He did. And did a bang-up job of it, according to Josh who carried on in a text. Something about *El Jefe*, whoever that is, being pleased with Owen's performance." Russ leaned over the bed. "How are you feeling this morning?"

"Like shit."

"It's no wonder. Between the surgery and the antibiotics they're pumping into you, if you weren't on your ass I'd be surprised."

"How long am I going to be on my ass?"

"I don't know. That's for the doctor to tell us when he gets here."

The nurse bustled in with what was supposed to be breakfast. Russ helped Wade sit up, and he was trying to gag down some godawful broth and flavorless gelatin squares when his mother and siblings came in carrying a takeout sack.

Oscar took one look at his breakfast tray and grimaced. "All that money for a hospital room and that's the best they can do? For what they're charging your insurance, you ought to be getting a rib-eye."

"That's okay. I couldn't gag it down anyway."

His mother kissed him and the girls gave him gentle hugs. "How are you feeling?"

"Like sh—" He glanced over at the girls. "Let's just say, I've been better."

"In other words, like shit," Oscar said cheerfully.

Wade let out with a crack of laughter that had pain lancing across his severed muscles. "Shit, that hurts," he moaned.

His mother looked at them and shook her head. She settled the kids on the futon and passed out breakfast sandwiches and hash browns. Wade sipped the horrible broth while they made short work of their fast-food breakfasts. He looked from his mom to Russ, wondering if they were as conscious as he was of the elephant in the room. They didn't act like anything was wrong. They didn't act as though anything had changed. But there wasn't much they could say or do with the three kids in the room. Oscar was fifteen and would understand, but they didn't need to be talking in front of the girls.

He hoped to hell they weren't acting in front of the kids. He hoped to hell he hadn't killed his mother's love for him yesterday morning.

Wade finally gave up on the broth and pushed the tray away. The family finished with their breakfast, and his mother was gathering up the wrappers and napkins when an older, tired-looking man in golf clothes walked in carrying an iPad.

"Good morning. You're looking better today, Mr. Baxter."

Wade took a peek at the man's nametag. "Dr. Perez. So you're the man responsible for the embroidery on my gut."

"That would be me. If the rest of you will excuse us, I need to look at Mr. Baxter's incision."

Mom and Russ herded the kids out. The doctor examined the long, red incision with its train-track parade of staples and the nasty-looking tube coming out of one end.

"You let this go too long," Dr. Perez chided. "If you'd come in even a day sooner, you'd have a couple of laparoscopic incisions and be headed back to work by the end of the week. As it is, you're going to be tethered to an IV for the better part of the week, and off work until after Christmas."

"What about doing the show? I'm the lead in the Durango Christmas production."

Dr. Perez gave him a *you've-got-to-be-kidding* look. "I hope you have a good understudy. You won't be back there, either."

Thank God he had a good understudy. Owen would have the lead now.

The doctor finished his examination and his family trooped back in the room. He gave them the discouraging news. "I won't be able to go back to work until after Christmas," he said forlornly. "Or do the show."

"Hey, man, a month of vacation. Too bad you hurt too much to enjoy it." Oscar's eyes danced with devilment.

"Thank you, Oscar."

"I wouldn't worry about the job. As long as highway construction takes, you won't have missed much," Russ teased.

Wade grinned weakly and shot him the finger.

"And you don't have to worry about the show," Mom added. "Josh texted me last night and said Owen did great. Whoever *El Jefe* is, he was impressed."

Wade smiled in relief. "*El Jefe's* the one with all the money."

"Ahh. I talked to Owen this morning. He's already agreed to step in until you can come back. I guess he'll have to finish the run," she told him.

"I hope he doesn't mind too much."

"He didn't sound like he minded. He's really a good-looking man when those scars are covered."

"What does he look like?"

Mom got out her phone and scrolled to a picture. Wade took the phone from her and stared at the image of a perfect Owen.

"My God, he's handsome. No wonder the scars bother him so much." He handed the phone back to his mother. "I guess they won't bother him anymore. Thanks, Mom. I don't know why I didn't think of it myself."

"Because you're a guy, dude. We don't think of stuff like that." Oscar said.

Wade winced. A gay guy might have. But Russ and Angie laughed like their feelings for him hadn't changed at all.

Maybe they hadn't.

"He is quite handsome. And as nice as they come," Angie said warmly. "He offered to come stay with you when you get out of the hospital. He says he works from home and he can set up his laptop on your dining room table. I hate not to be here, though."

"It's all right. You've got three kids at home who need you. And Owen will take care of me."

"I'm sure he will." Russ chuckled. "And on that note, we need to get on the road. Between the construction and the Christmas traffic, it's going to take us awhile to drive back."

The kids all said their farewells. Russ shook his hand and made him promise to call his mother every day with an update. He herded the kids out of the room, leaving her alone with Wade.

There were tears in her eyes as she took his hand. "I love you, honey. Nothing in this world will ever change that." She leaned down and kissed his cheek. "We'll talk whenever you're ready." She paused a minute. "And talk to Owen. He really cares for you."

"I love you, too. And I will. I promise."

Wade watched through tearful eyes as his mother smiled at him and left the room.

What a wonderful mother. She now knew how the Baxter had come out in him. She now knew how ugly he was. And she loved him anyway.

***

Wade sat curled up on the sofa and tried to concentrate on the bestseller he'd ordered this morning on his e-reader. But the pages kept blurring together, and for the life of him he couldn't follow the convoluted plot.

After he'd read page forty for the third time, he gave up and exited the book. His first impulse was to go to the shopping cart and look for something with a simpler plot, but he doubted ordering a different book would help. Between the oral antibiotics they'd given him and the pain pills he was still using, his concentration was shot. The most sensible thing to do would be to take a nap, but he'd slept away most of last week and was tired of sleeping. He longed to get up and do something, but the surgery and the abdominal infection caused by the rupture had taken such a huge toll, he was happy to be able to walk from one end of the house to the other. For the thousandth time, he wished he'd gotten medical help sooner. He'd be back on his feet by now. He'd be back at work, and, more importantly, back at the theater, singing and dancing to his heart's content.

Not that they needed him at the moment. Owen was playing J. Pierrepont Finch, and would be until the end of the run. According to everyone he'd talked to, his lover was doing a splendid job of it.

Wade's lips curled into a smile. Sure, he wished he was back up on the stage. But he couldn't be happier for Owen. It was high time he was where he was supposed to be, using his talent where it was meant to be used. There was a definite change in Owen these days. His step was lighter, his smile quicker. He radiated confidence in spades. This was the Owen Aldrete he was meant to be. Owen Aldrete always deserved more than an ugly Baxter in his life. Now more than ever.

Wade glanced over at the laptop on the dining room table. His mother had been right about Owen. He was as nice as they came. And he'd taken marvelous care of Wade. He'd come to the hospital that Sunday after doing the afternoon matinee, bearing homemade broth Miguel Abonce's mother had made.

Owen had insisted on staying that night and the next, until most of Wade's tethers were gone and he could get to the restroom by himself. Owen had driven Wade home the following Friday, and had moved into the spare bedroom. He'd put meals on the table and done laundry and designed his websites from his laptop, at Wade's dining room table. They'd talked a lot and laughed often. But Wade had avoided discussing the obvious, and Owen hadn't brought it up. They both sensed the talk needed to wait until Wade was feeling better.

If Wade had his way, they would postpone the discussion forever. But Owen wouldn't stand for that. And Wade had promised his mother he would level with his man. Sooner or later, he was going to have to share his ugly family secrets. After which he had no guarantee Owen would want him any longer.

Wade shuffled to the kitchen. He was finally getting his appetite back. What was left of the spaghetti casserole Rachel had dropped by this morning was calling his name. They had eaten some of it earlier, before Owen left for the theater. Wade dished up another generous portion and was sitting at the bar finishing it off when the doorbell rang. He pushed himself off the stool and hobbled to the door. He didn't know who'd be ringing his doorbell at nine on Friday night. All his friends were at the theater.

Well, maybe not all of them. He checked the peephole, then opened the door to a smiling Jason and Emily. They were dressed casually, and Emily carried a stack of paperbacks. "It's so good to see you. Where's your renegades?" he asked as he gave Emily's arm a squeeze.

Hugs still hurt.

Jason leaned forward and gave him a big fist bump. "We have a secret weapon. It's called a babysitter."

"The teenager across the street likes to make a little money so he can take his girlfriend out. We figure a guy sitter's probably better because he knows every stunt they're likely to pull," She laughed. Wade ushered them into the family room.

Emily piled the books on the coffee table. "Something to kill the time."

"Thanks. They will be read and appreciated. I'm glad you came. I'm going stir crazy."

He curled up on the sofa and Emily and Jason sat across from him.

"We figured tonight might be a good night to come because all your theater buddies are busy. Have a lot of them dropped by?" Jason asked.

"They've been great. Owen and I aren't the best in the kitchen. The Durango cooks have kept us in food."

"So how are you feeling? Really." Emily leaned forward.

"Still weak. Still sore. They finally pulled out the drain two days ago. The staples come out Monday. Owen's been a godsend."

"So I hear," Jason said. "He's also feeling guilty as hell. He feels like it's his fault you let it go so long. He said if he, and we, hadn't put you under so much stress about coming out to your mom and Russ, you would have caught on sooner that you were sick. Quite a session we had in the support group this week."

"I hope you all told him what a load of crap that was," Wade said.

"Tried to."

"He," she pointed at Jason, "came home feeling just as guilty," Emily said. "It was the other folks in the support group who told them both to get their heads out of their asses. Anyway, how did the talk with your mom go? Owen said you were out to them now."

"Talk? You have to be kidding. They found out because I was half out of it and laid a big, juicy one on Owen on the way out the door to the O.R." She cracked up. "Damn it, Emily, it's not funny," he snapped.

"And when you did talk?" Jason prompted.

"We never did. They had to get back. They had the kids with them. All Mom said was that we would talk whenever I was ready. That I really needed to talk to Owen." He sighed. "And I do. But I'm scared to death. I don't want him to know the Baxter stories. I'm afraid he's not going to want me when he finds out."

Emily and Jason were silent for a minute. "Did your mother seem upset at knowing the truth about you?" Emily asked.

"She didn't act like it. Neither did Russ. But I haven't really talked to them so I don't know."

"Come on, man. She's your mom," Jason chided. "If she was pissed or upset, believe me, you'd know."

"So it stands to reason that if Angie and Russ were okay learning about your being gay, Owen's going to be equally understanding about the fucked-up Baxters," Emily said.

"And even if he's not, you need to be honest with him if you're ever going to have more than a casual relationship with the man," Jason added.

"I know. But do you have any idea how hard it's going to be? Telling him all that shit?"

"Why?" Emily asked. "Absolutely none of it was your fault. It's not your fault you were born into that kind of crap."

"I know that. But the Baxter blood runs through my veins. And there's not a damned thing I can do about it."

Emily started to say more, but they heard a key in the lock and Owen came striding in, still in his stage makeup. It took Wade's breath away how handsome Owen was. He leaned down and gave Wade a warm, sweet kiss on the mouth before shaking hands with Jason and hugging Emily. Jason and Emily told Owen how much they'd enjoyed the performance they'd seen last week, and then conversation veered to things at the theater.

Emily and Jason left an hour later. Owen wandered into the kitchen and came out in a few minutes with a plate of Rachel's casserole. He sat in the chair Jason had vacated and propped his feet on the coffee table. "The three of you were looking mighty serious when I walked in," he observed.

"We were talking about something heavy," Wade admitted.

"Your mom and Russ?"

"In part. And you."

Owen's fork stopped halfway to his mouth. "Me? They already knew about me."

"They think I should level with you about my family. Mom thinks so too. She made me promise I'd talk with you."

"What I don't understand is why talking to me is such a problem."

"Because when you learn the truth about my family, you're not going to want me anymore. You come from a nice family and don't understand."

Owen looked him in the eye. "Try me."

Wade took a deep breath. The time had come. Owen would either understand or he wouldn't.

"Okay. You've met my uncles, the loudmouthed drunk and the quietly homophobic racist. They're mild compared to Buck and Molly."

"Who are Buck and Molly?"

"My father and grandmother who are both dead and I hope are burning in a special place in hell."

"Harsh."

"With damn good reason." He paused a minute. "We'll start with Buck. He managed to run off my birth mother when I was about two. When I was six, we happened on a beautiful girl selling cosmetics in a Kentucky department store. I fell in love with that girl. And she fell in love with me."

"Angie. Your mom."

"My mom. Anyway, Buck charmed her and married her. I don't know if she loved him, but she loved me enough to marry him. And he didn't let her see his bad side. The mean streak. She didn't know what he was really like until it was too late."

"Shit."

"Shit's right. Anyway, he brought her home to Verde. She got a job at the hair salon. He went to work as a deputy sheriff and tried to make a go of a small ranch. Wasn't much good at either. When he'd get upset, he'd hit the bottle. And then he'd hit her. She put up with it because she had no legal claim to me. She loved me and wasn't willing to leave me to Buck's tender mercies."

"Jesus," Owen breathed softly.

"Anyway, it all came to a head when I was ten. I tried to stop him one night. He picked me up and threw me into a wall. Broke my arm in three places and fractured my skull."

"The scars," Owen said.

Wade ran his hand down his left arm. "The damned thing still aches when it's raining."

"He went to jail for battering a minor. He got the maximum sentence with no possibility of parole. Molly, my grandmother, was distraught. She and my uncles blamed Mom for what Buck did to me."

"That makes no sense."

"They're Baxters. That's all it takes. Anyway, Molly and my uncles were even more upset when Mom petitioned for permanent custody and got it. The shit really hit the fan when Buck signed away his parental rights and Mom adopted me."

"Why were they so upset?"

"To them, blood is everything. Mom and I have no blood ties. Never mind that she's the best damned mother on the planet. I was a Baxter. I had their blood in my veins and I should have gone to them."

"I see."

"It didn't help that by then I hated being a Baxter and made no secret of it. I hated my father with a passion and refused to go see him in prison, even after we learned he was dying."

"Ouch. So is that the story?"

"I'm barely getting started."

"Okay."

Wade took a minute to gather his thoughts. "Fast forward ten years. I'm a senior in college, Mom's started her own business, life's finally good for her. Among my father's other sins, he was cheating on Mom with jailbait. Stupid girl was waiting for Buck to get out of prison. Word gets back to Verde that Buck's terminally ill. Again they blame Mom, this time for Buck dying in prison. The jailbait teamed up with her brother and Molly and tried to destroy Mom's brand-new business. Damn near succeeded. And when that wasn't enough, Molly decided she was taking away the thing in life Mom loved most."

Owen looked up sharply. "Which would be you?"

"Which would be me." Wade gulped. "She had a gun on me, Owen. She was going to shoot me. And would have if Mom hadn't pushed me out of the way and taken the bullet herself." He stopped and wiped his eyes. "She shot Mom and then shot herself. She died right in front of me. Mom damn near bled out. She would have died if the bullet had been one fucking inch over."

"Holy shit." Owen put the untouched plate of food down on the coffee table.

"My *grandmother* would have killed me to spite Mom. She would have murdered her own blood kin. The kin she thought was so damn important." His eyes filled again. "That's what I come from, Owen. That's the blood that runs through my veins."

Owen was quiet a minute. "I realize you might not have an answer for this, but I'm going to ask it anyway. You keep talking about how your being gay equates with your being ugly like the Baxters. Why are they so linked in your mind? Or do you know?"

"Oh, hell yeah, I know. Benny said so."

"Who is Benny?"

"Benny Keller. My best friend from the time I was six. Or he was, until he broke my nose and threw me out of our apartment." They sat silent for a minute. "By the time all the shit went down that summer with Molly, I knew damned well I wasn't into girls. I was pretty certain I was gay but wanted to know for sure. The evening after Buck's funeral, I didn't go straight back to College Station. I went to an Austin gay bar and picked up a guy. By morning, I knew for a fact I was gay. I drove back to school and tried to talk to Benny. I thought he'd understand."

"Instead, he beat the shit out of you."

"Broke my nose. Screamed at me that I was as fucked up as the rest of the family. He said we were a bad lot, period, and that he was done with me. By the time I got back from the emergency room, he'd piled all my stuff on the front porch and changed the locks. I had to spend the night in a motel." He stopped and took a deep breath. "I never told anyone else that I'm gay except Sandra. I figured secrecy was better than losing my friends and my family. If

Benny thought I was fucked up and exactly like the Baxters, so would they."

"So you're telling me that because Benny equated your being gay with being ugly like the Baxters, you feel the same way."

"What the hell else am I supposed to think?"

"That Benny's full of shit."

"Maybe he is. The bottom line is that gay or straight, I'm a Baxter. The Baxters are a damned ugly bunch. There's not one of us that's not fucked up in some way or another. If I weren't gay, it would be coming out another way. That's why I never wanted to tell you about my family and my past. If you didn't know, you could go on believing I'm good. But now you know the truth. And you'd be crazy to want me, knowing what you know." He cursed the tears pooling in his eyes. "You can do better than me, Owen. You'd be foolish not to."

Owen sat back a minute. "So the bottom line is that you think because you're a Baxter, you're bad. The bad comes out in you as gay. If you weren't gay, it would be coming out some other way. Baxter blood runs through your veins and there's nothing you can do about it."

"Pretty much."

"Would it do any good for me to point out how utterly fucked up that line of reasoning is?"

"It's not fucked up in the least. It's what it is."

"No, it's not what it is. It's what you've built it up in your head to be. The only thing that's ugly about you is the horrible damage your family has done to your heart and your soul. And that you've let them do it."

Wade's eyes flashed. "I haven't 'let' them do anything."

"Yeah, you have. You've bought into your family's belief that blood is everything. That because you carry their blood, you're as bad as they are."

"I am as bad as they are," Wade murmured. "You don't want to see it, but I am."

"No, you're not. But I could argue with you all day and you're not going to believe it because you choose not to." He threw up his hands. "You want to go on thinking ill of yourself, I can't stop you. I'll be damned if I waste my breath arguing about it." He stood and went to his laptop. "I'm at a loss. I'm not a counselor or a therapist, and I don't know what to say other than you're being utterly ridiculous." He powered down the computer. "I can't help you. I'm not even going to try. But you had damn well better get a counselor and a good one. You need one."

"I don't need counseling."

"Oh yeah, you do. You need to sit down with a therapist and work out your feelings. About being gay and about being a Baxter. If you don't, you're never going to accept yourself. You're never going to be okay with being gay. And that is the one thing I absolutely cannot live with."

"You can't live with knowing the truth about me, you mean."

"No, that's not what I mean. That's what you insist on hearing."

Wade watched silently as Owen shoved the computer in his backpack along with the mouse and the connecting wires. He disappeared for a few minutes before returning with his duffel bag. He leaned down and gave Wade a tender kiss on his lips. "Please, Wade. Get the help you need. Get your head on straight."

Wade looked at Owen through tear-filled eyes. "Is this it?" he asked softly.

"Not necessarily. Get your head on straight, and I'll be back."

Owen picked up his bags and walked out the door. Wade sat frozen for a few minutes. Enraged, he picked up Owen's plate of spaghetti and threw it across the room. The plate hit the wall and exploded into a thousand pieces, spaghetti and sticky red sauce running down the wall and staining the carpet. Owen had heard his story and had run for his life.

So much for telling the truth, he thought bitterly as he stared at the mess he'd made. So much for leveling with Owen. He'd opened up his family's can of ugly, and Owen had fled like a scalded cat. Owen didn't do ugly. Unlike Wade's mother, who'd seen him for what he was and loved him anyway, Owen had taken one look at the real Wade Baxter and ran. He hadn't even argued. He'd thrown out the universal "get some-counseling" recommendation, and gotten out of Dodge.

Wade sighed, got up and went to the kitchen, then wiped down the wall with a soapy rag, wincing at the red stains that would have to be painted over. He picked up the larger pieces of glass, and, holding his side, ran the sweeper over the rug to get the smaller ones.

He knew better than to put any stock in Owen's, "I'll be back." That promise was contingent on Wade "getting his head on straight." Even if Owen meant what he said, he wouldn't be back. Because Wade's head wasn't on straight, and never would be.

He was a Baxter.

And Baxters never had their heads on straight.

CHAPTER 15

It was time for a change of scene.

Wade threw some clothes in a duffel and packed a Dopp Kit. Josh had driven him to the doctor this morning to have his staples removed, and Dr. Perez had cleared him to drive short distances. He was off the painkillers and was down to four antibiotic pills a day.

Physically, he was doing fine. Not quite up to returning to work, but not housebound anymore. He knew Heaven's Point was a lot farther than the short distances the doctor suggested, but one more day alone in his quiet house and he would be screaming. He couldn't stay here where he would repeatedly relive their last talk before Owen had packed his things and walked out of Wade's life.

In deference to the doctor's restrictions on lifting, he packed his clothes and groceries in small bags and carried them one at a time to the truck. He left his neighbor a note to please get his mail for him, and turned the heat down to fifty-five. He had to sit a minute to get his breath before putting the truck in gear.

It'll be good to get out of town. He drove by the increasingly abundant Christmas decorations adorning San Antonio homes and businesses. In the past, Christmas had been one of his favorite holidays, but this year, the place in his heart that harbored wreaths and Santas, peace and goodwill was empty, and he would give anything to fast-forward to January and be done with it.

Traffic was light once he got past San Antonio. But there seemed to be no getting away from Christmas. The small towns were festooned with trees and Santas, and all manner of holiday trimmings. Marble Falls had their light display set up, and Burnet sported big signs advertising Main Street Bethlehem. The full-time residents of Heaven's Point were mostly elderly and not up to a lot of decorating, but he could count on Holly and Jimmy Adamcik going all out doing up their big, lakefront home.

He turned onto the farm market road that circled the lake, which sparkled in the December sunlight, a cool breeze ruffling the water's surface. It was warm enough that he could lower the windows and breathe in the tangy, fishy smell he'd always associated with the lake and the little house, a couple of streets off the water, where his mother had raised him. He wasn't exactly smiling as he clattered over the cattle guard leading into Heaven's Point, but he felt something loosen in his chest.

For better or worse, he was home.

He drove into the tiny lake village and passed several streets before turning. He had the keys to two houses on his key ring, and could stay in either one. He almost stopped at the one Gran and Gramps owned. It was bigger and had a view of the beachfront park and the lake. Instead, he drove a little further down and turned into the driveway of a small two-bedroom cottage. He stared at the little house and let the memories flow.

The day he and his mom walked through the front door for the first time, he was a scared ten-year-old clinging desperately to the hand of his young stepmother.

Their first Christmas together in the little house had only a few gifts under the tree, but so much love.

The day they'd come home with Judge Riley's signature on the documents that made them mother and son officially.

The cakes his mother had made for him to celebrate and to comfort, and sometimes just because.

The horrible afternoon Molly Baxter had shot his mother in the living room.

The afternoon he'd escorted his beautiful mother down to the beach and given her away in marriage to Russ.

He carried his groceries and his clothes inside. Unloading the truck had tired him, so he sat in the living room to catch his breath. His eyes flicked around the room. He liked the simple blue sofa and dove gray carpet, which had magically appeared after the shooting.

This room had changed, and for the better. But the rest of the house was pretty much as it had been when he grew up in it. There were times he wondered why his mother held onto it after she and Russ moved out to the vineyard. Tonight, he was sincerely glad she had.

His phone buzzed and a text from his mother appeared.

Your truck in driveway?

He grinned and shook his head. It sure hadn't taken long for one of the neighbors to spot him.

He texted back: *Yeah. Okay if I stay a few days?*

Sure. Want to come for dinner?

Wade thought a minute. *Tomorrow night?*

His mother sent a smiley face.

He found the golf cart in its usual corner of the garage. It was clean. Probably Oscar and the girls had used it recently. The little beach park was deserted but for a family of ducks swimming offshore. Wade parked on the packed sand and let the cold air blow in his face. The shadows lengthened as the afternoon passed, and the sun dropped lower in the sky. Still, Wade sat and stared out at the water.

He needed this. He needed home. He needed the comfort of his childhood. The irony wasn't lost on him. Heaven's Point was the last place he could be himself. But he still needed the comfort the little community offered him.

Damn if he knew why.

***

Wade sat at the dining room table and stared at the computer screen in consternation. He had no idea what Jodi would like for Christmas. Or Melanie either, come to think of it. He'd never been a seven-year-old girl or a ten-year-old girl. He hadn't had any sisters or girl cousins. His friends had all been guys. Even living with Noelle hadn't taught him much.

Young females were a mystery to him.

He looked up gifts for girls and scrolled down a baffling selection of dolls and shoes and backpacks and purses, mostly pink and sparkly. God help the tomboys. There wasn't much out there for them. He settled on pink backpacks to house their new iPads, and was about to look for something travel-related to put with Oscar's yellow luggage when he heard a vehicle in the driveway and spotted his mom and Russ getting out.

His mother was carrying a sack from the local café, the sight of which made his mouth water. He pushed his laptop to one side and made it to the door before they even knocked. "To what do I owe the pleasure of this visit?" he said as he hugged his mother. "I saw you last night. And the night before that."

"And the night before that," Russ chimed in. "Between feeding you and Oscar every night, I'm going broke."

"Aw, shut up. You pack it in pretty good yourself. It's good to have Wade here." She handed Wade the sack. "I got us burgers. The pork chops haven't been the same since Gus retired."

"Gus retired? When?"

Mom thought for a minute. "Back in October, I think. Lisa's having a hell of a time replacing him. She said to tell you that Benny would be home on the twentieth and would be staying with her and Rory if you wanted to come by and see him."

Wade nodded, not willing to ruin her appetite or his with an explanation of why he wouldn't be seeing Benny. He poured them each a glass of iced tea while his mother found plates and Russ knives and forks. They gathered around the table and made quick work of the hamburgers. "That was good," Wade said. "Whoever she's got working today, she needs to keep them."

"I agree." Mom smiled gently at him. "It's good to have you close. But are you all right here? Would you rather be out at the vineyard?"

"I'm not kicking Oscar out of his room. That boy's had enough sleeping three to a bed. He needs his own space, not bunking with me or his little sisters."

"We need to add on another wing." Russ sighed.

"I'd kill for a house the size of that place you're renting," Mom said. "Which is way too big since Sandra and Noelle left. Or are you sharing it with Owen now?"

Wade shook his head. "I'm not sharing it with Owen." He willed his voice to stay calm. "Owen and I aren't an item anymore."

Mom and Russ looked at one another, clearly uncertain. "You can ask, Mom. Doesn't matter if it's a guy I broke up with, you can still ask."

"What happened? He seemed so nice."

"I liked him," Russ added.

"I talked to him like you told me to do. I told him about the Baxters. The shit with Buck and the shit with Molly. And he rabbited. He got out of there so fast it made my head swim."

Their faces fell. "That surprises me," Russ said. "He didn't seem like the kind who'd run."

"Me, too. What did he say to you?" Mom asked.

"He said he couldn't help me. He said he wasn't a counselor and that I needed one. He said he'd be back when I got my head on straight."

"And how may I ask is your head on crooked?" she asked.

"Isn't it obvious? I'm a Baxter. Every damned Baxter's head is on crooked. Every damned one of us is ugly. Benny took great pleasure in pointing that out to me the afternoon I told him I'm gay, and he broke my nose because of it."

"I guess you won't be taking Lisa up on her invitation," Russ commented dryly.

"You got that right."

"That jackass," Mom snapped. "So you told Owen about the illustrious Baxter clan and said that you think you're as bad as they are. Did he agree that you're bad?"

"No. He said my thinking's fucked up and I'm being ridiculous, and that unless I straighten it out, I'll never be able to accept myself as a gay man. He said he couldn't live with that."

Russ and Mom winced.

"So he out and out dumped you. Shitty of him." Her eyes shot sparks.

"He said he'd be back if I ever got my head on straight. Which, being a Baxter, isn't likely to happen. So I guess I've lost him forever." He wadded up his napkin and threw it across the room, making a perfect shot into the trashcan. "It's all right. I don't know what he thought he wanted with me, anyway. He can do so much better."

"Aw, no, Wade. That's not true. You're the best of the best," Mom said. "He's not going to do one bit better than you."

"You're biased."

"Maybe she is, but I'm not," Russ said. "You're a fine man. You're not like the rest of that asshole family. You never were. And you never will be."

"I am gay," he pointed out.

"So?" they said in unison.

"We would care because?" Mom asked.

"You really don't mind?" he asked softly.

"It's who you are," Russ said. "Wade, neither your mom nor I were born yesterday. We've suspected for a long time, but we never said anything because it doesn't matter to us. You're still you. Okay?"

"Okay." He looked at them and smiled through his tears. "I got lucky with the two of you."

"Yes, you did," Russ agreed. "Especially her." He put out his hand for a fist bump.

Wade bumped his fist. "I really did."

"If I can risk spoiling this kumbaya moment," Russ stated, "although Owen's actions leave a lot to be desired, he's right about one thing. It probably wouldn't hurt for you to talk to a professional. Go back to Dr. Jacobsen. Or find someone in San Antonio. Sometimes a counselor can say the right thing to help you understand when all family and friends do is stick their feet in their mouths."

"Russ is right. You need to talk to someone. And soon." She nailed him with her Mom-knows-best expression, and he found himself nodding.

They helped Wade clean off the table and load the dishwasher. He stood at the door and watched them drive away. They were such good people. They accepted him completely. More than he accepted himself. And his mother was determined to see the best in him. But even her love wasn't going to change him. He was a Baxter. As fucked up as the rest of them. And all the love and acceptance in the world wasn't going to change that one little bit.

***

Owen smiled and bowed to yet another standing ovation from his appreciative audience. This Sunday matinee was the last performance of *How to Succeed* and Owen felt almost wistful as he took his final bows. It had been wonderful getting back up on the stage and singing and dancing.

With every performance, his confidence had grown. He could still do it. He could entertain a crowd. He could bring people to their feet, whistling and cheering and stomping in appreciation. It felt good. It felt right. He hadn't realized how badly he'd missed it until he was back in front of an audience. And he was staying in front of an audience. He wasn't waiting five years to sing and dance again.

The cast trooped to the lobby to greet their patrons. By the time the cast returned to the dressing room, the crew was already taking the props and smaller set pieces to the upstairs storage.

Owen put the J. Pierrepont costumes together on the rack so the costumer could pick them up tomorrow and catalogue them into her warehouse, where they would be stored until needed for another production. He put on his jeans and a long-sleeved tee and washed off the stage makeup in the restroom, his scars re-emerging as the concealer ran down the drain. He wiped his face with a towel and looked in the mirror. The scars were as bad as ever. But they no longer bothered him. He could cover them up when he needed to, and the rest of the time… to hell with them.

He rounded up his coat and was on his way out when Josh bounced in the dressing room with Maggie Gutierrez, their developmental director. They were both smiling broadly. "Wanted to let you know, the Navarros bestowed upon us another substantial contribution. Maggie's sister dropped off the check herself a few minutes ago. Merry Christmas to us."

The dressing room erupted into cheers.

Josh pointed to Owen and motioned him out the door. "I wanted to remind you of *El Jefe*'s request the night he met you. He wants you front and center again."

Owen's chest swelled. "What's the next production?"

"*Oklahoma*. Auditions are the middle of January."

It was already the twenty-third of December. The middle of January was coming up fast. Owen thought a minute. "You haven't cast any of the roles yet?" Josh shook his head.

"I'd play any role you wanted to cast me in, but you have younger actors for your two leads. I'd have fun doing Ali Hakim. Or, I do a bad guy really well."

Josh cocked his head and looked at him. "Jud Fry. You'd be playing against type, but I can see it. I'll email you the exact date."

"I'll be there."

Owen headed for the back door, his euphoria fading a bit as he walked toward his car. He would most certainly be there for the audition. He wondered if Wade would be there too. But he couldn't ask him. Wade had been on radio silence since Owen had walked away. He'd hadn't seen or heard from his troubled young lover since the night Wade told his horrific story.

In retrospect, Owen realized that walking out on Wade that night hadn't been the smart thing to do, especially when Wade was hurting so badly. But Owen had been honest. He was at an absolute loss when it came to Wade's thinking. He had no idea what to say or do to make things better. He had no idea how to help Wade break his twisted mindset. There was no way he could be with a man who couldn't accept being gay, even if he loved Wade with all his heart.

So he had done the chickenshit thing and run away.

But he missed Wade. So much that sometimes it took his breath away.

He was almost to the car when Sophie caught up with him. Letti was a few feet behind her.

"Daddy, we're going to the pizza place for an early supper. Want to come?"

"Do I have to endure your mother's gimlet gaze while I munch on my pepperoni?" he teased as Letti walked up.

"I think I can restrain myself for the forty-five minutes it'll take us to eat," Letti said dryly. "Come on. I'll even spring for the beer."

They left their cars in the parking lot and walked down the block to the pizza place. Most of the cast showed up, even mean girl Hailey and her boyfriend. Soon the corner they'd commandeered was overflowing with beer and pizza and high spirits.

Owen cheerfully killed half a pizza and drank a couple of beers. The dancing he'd done as J. Pierrepont Finch had taken off a few pounds, and if he did Oklahoma, he would be dancing again and would burn off any calories he indulged in over the holidays. He wondered how soon Wade would be up to dancing on stage. Probably already was, as quickly as the young bounced back.

The sun had already set and the wind had picked up when he and Letti walked out of the pizza parlor. Sophie had stayed behind with friends, who promised to drive her home. "Are you still on for New Year's with the kids?" she asked. Letti got them for Christmas every other year, and this was her year. He would pick them up on the twenty-seventh and have them until school started.

"I am. I thought we'd go to the big party downtown. Why? You got a hot date?"

Letti turned her nose up. "One of Mama's endless blind dates. Gotta marry off that divorced daughter before she gets too old to catch a man."

Owen winced. "Sorry about that."

"I hope Wade doesn't mind having the kids along that night."

"He likes the kids." Owen hoped she'd let the topic of Wade pass.

No such luck. "I'm surprised he didn't come see you perform," she said as he shut the door behind them. "Or is he still pretty sick?"

"I don't know. I haven't seen him in a while."

Letti looked at him with surprise. "You haven't? I thought you'd moved in to help him. I thought you two were serious."

"We were. We're not anymore."

"Color me astonished. What the hell happened?"

Owen took a deep breath. "He's never going to have his head on straight. He'll never be able to accept himself as a gay man, and I can't live with that."

Letti looked at him sharply. "What makes you think he'll never be able to accept himself? It looks to me like he accepts himself, and as far as having his head on straight, he's the most level-headed young man I've ever met."

"He isn't. He doesn't. Not really. It's all tied up with that family he comes from."

"His mom and her husband? Oh, the uncles. Did he explain why they have him so tied up?"

"It's a horrible story."

"I can do horrible."

They walked slowly down the sidewalk while Owen told Letti Wade's story. She listened silently as he told her of Wade's troubled childhood and the things his father and grandmother had done. "And then when he told his best friend he was gay, the asshole broke his nose and told him he was as evil and ugly as the rest of the Baxters. So he has it in his mind that he's no better than they are, that in him the ugliness comes out as homosexuality, and no amount of arguing is going to change his mind."

"So what did you say to him?"

"I told him to get some counseling and to get his head on straight."

Letti skidded to a stop and looked at him disbelievingly. "You did *what?*"

"What I said. I told him I couldn't help him. I told him to get some counseling. I told him I'd be back when he got his head on straight."

"I can't believe you." Letti moved to him, her eyes shooting sparks. "You. Are. An. *Asshole.*" She poked her finger into his chest. "A *pendejo.*" She poked him again. "A jerk. A turd. The most selfish jackass I've ever known." She turned away in disgust. "I thought you were an asshat for divorcing me. What you did to me doesn't compare to what you did to Wade. Jesus, Owen. What the fuck kind of self-centered shit are you, anyway?"

Owen stared at her in shock. "Hang on a damn minute," he ground out. "Asshole? Jerk? Self-centered shit? Where do you get off calling me that?"

"Because you *are,*" Letti snapped. "Listen to yourself. Wade's story has to be the most traumatic I've ever heard. His father damn near killed him, and his grandmother tried to. Then his best friend threw them up to him when he tried to come out. And all you can think to do is tell him you'll be back when he gets his head on straight and walk out on him because *you* have a problem with his issues. *Hijole.* When did everything in this world become about you?"

"What the hell was I supposed to do? I'm not a shrink. I don't have a fucking clue what he needs. I don't know what to say to him. And yeah, it pisses the hell out of me that he won't accept himself, that he's bought into their way of thinking."

She shook her head. "Selfish, selfish, selfish. I'm disappointed in you. Sure, he bought into their way of thinking. They preached it to him from the time he was little. Won't accept himself? Maybe he can't accept himself. What's he supposed to do? Snap his fingers and suddenly the blinders come off? That kind of thinking takes years of counseling to overcome. And, *asshole,* someone who loves him enough to support him while he goes through it."

She looked at him like he'd grown another nose. "You know what? He may never be over the trauma, as sensitive as Wade is and as deeply as his emotions run." She stopped and took a breath. "That so-called friend has a lot to answer for. Wade might never have associated being gay with being an ugly Baxter if his friend hadn't said what he did. And what do you think you did to him? Hell, you probably set him back that much more. You as much as told him he wasn't good enough for you the way he is."

Owen's head spun at Letti's brutal honesty. She was right. That's exactly what he had done. His actions had said it the loudest, most definite way possible that Wade wasn't good enough for him. Since Wade couldn't accept himself fully, Owen couldn't either. Guilt and shame washed over him as he remembered the look in Wade's eyes when he walked out the door.

"Shit," he whispered. "What have I done?"

Letti looked up at his scarred face. "The question you need to ask yourself is what have you become. You've changed. Those scars changed more than the landscape on your face. You've become selfish. Self-centered. Self-absorbed. You only think of yourself. How everything is going to make you feel. You still aren't stepping up to the plate with Marco, and Sophie has to make you be the father she needs. As far as you're concerned, it's your way or the highway. You're so damn hot to see every gay man come out of the closet, you don't stop to think that sometimes a gay man has good reason for keeping his sexuality private. And you've let Wade down, maybe worse than anyone else in his life. Maybe he's not the man you need. But you sure haven't been the man he needs either."

Owen stood silent as the tirade sunk in. Letti's words cut like knives. She nailed it. He had changed, and not for the better. He'd let his children down. He'd let Wade down.

He looked at her, helplessly. "You're right. I'm not the man Wade needs. I can't be. I don't know what to say or do to make him feel better about himself."

"Maybe it's not your job to say anything. That's the job of the counselor he needs to talk to. But there's plenty you can do."

"Such as?"

"Be there for him. Help him get the therapy he needs. Make the appointments and take him yourself if you have to. Support him and encourage him and, damn it, love him the way he is and not the way you think he should be. Accept him as he is, even when he can't accept himself. That would mean you'd have to put him and his feelings above your own, if you can even do that at this point." She gripped his arm. "I understand why you had to let me down. But there's no reason you have to let him down, too. So, damn it, put on your big boy boxers and be the man he needs you to be."

"Jesus. Why don't you tell me what you really think?"

"What do you want me to do? Sugarcoat it and have you miss the point? Damn it, Owen, I'm trying to get through to you. I love Wade, and, fool that I am, I still love you. Wade's been good for you. I'm trying to get you to see how to be as good for him. But if you're going to do that, you're going to have to decide two things. First, is he worth it?"

"And the second thing?"

"You have to decide if you can be the man he needs. It's not going to be easy."

"And if I can't?"

"Then back the hell off and let him find a man who can."

Owen gulped. "I guess I have some thinking to do."

"I guess you do."

He smiled ruefully. "You always could deliver a carefully aimed kick in the pants."

"I aim to please."

They walked in silence to their cars.

Owen drove home, deep in thought. He took the stairs two at a time and settled on the sofa with an e-reader he didn't bother to turn on. He gazed down at the empty screen. Letti's questions circled around in his head. Was Wade worth it? And could he be the man Wade needed him to be?

The first question was easy. Of course Wade was worth it. His smile. His laughter. His enormous talent. The way he felt in Owen's arms. The way he gave his love. Wade loved him. Wade saw the man behind the scars. Wade had dragged him out of his self-imposed exile and forced him to rejoin the land of the living. Wade had done so much for him.

Could he do the same? Could he be the man Wade needed him to be?

Yeah, I can.

Or he would die trying.

Owen grabbed his car keys and sprinted out the door. He jumped in the car and peeled out of the parking lot, making a beeline for Wade's house.

He would love Wade even if Wade couldn't love himself.

Owen pulled into Wade's driveway. The house was dark but for the front porch light. The garage was shut tight. He rang the doorbell twice, but no lights came on and no one came to the door.

Wade wasn't there. He would try again tomorrow. He supposed he could call or text. But he didn't want to take the chance that Wade would hang up on him or block his texts. Besides, this kind of talk needed to happen face to face.

Owen turned around and was on his way to the car when a truck pulled into the driveway next door and a young couple got out.

"Looking for Wade?" the woman asked.

"Yeah."

"He's out of town. We've been getting his mail for the last week and a half."

"Marcie, hush," the husband chided her.

"He's not casing the joint. I've seen his car over here a lot."

Owen smiled. "I am definitely not casing the joint." He introduced himself to the couple. "Do you have any idea where Wade's gone?"

The couple looked at one another. The husband shrugged. "I don't have a clue," Marcie said. "All the note said was that he'd be gone until after Christmas."

Owen thanked the couple. After Christmas. That was a pretty good clue. Wade loved his family. The Riley family. He was probably somewhere in their vicinity.

Owen got in the car and looked up Heaven's Point, and then Verde Vineyards. He threw the phone on the dash and stopped at the closest filling station to gas up before going home and packing a duffel.

CHAPTER 16

Wade stared at the screen of his laptop. Over a hundred emails had piled up since he'd gone through them last. He deleted the promotional and social media entries with one click of the mouse and started with the personal, which he would read one by one. He'd slept late and filled his stomach with a big bowl of sugar-laden cereal, which would hold him until dinner tonight at his mother's. Despite Russ's teasing, they insisted he eat supper with them every night, which he found a welcome respite from his daytime isolation. Isolation that was growing lonelier by the day.

An email from Josh reminded him that auditions for *Oklahoma* were coming up soon. Wade loved the vintage classic. He wasn't interested in playing Curly McLain, which was written for a baritone or a bass, but he would absolutely love to play Will Parker, the other lead, which was written for a tenor. But it would most likely mean facing Owen again.

After Mr. Navarro's request, he'd bet his pickup truck that Owen would be cast in the play also. He would be acting with Owen, singing with Owen, and up on the stage with Owen. And then he would be going home alone.

He cursed sharply and slammed down the laptop lid. He'd come up here trying to outrun the pain. Instead, he'd brought it with him. He'd never missed anyone in his life the way he did Owen. But Owen had left, unable to cope with his issues. As much as he hated admitting it, leaving was probably the wisest thing Owen could have done. The man he loved deserved a better man than he could ever be.

Owen deserved better than a Baxter.

Restless, he grabbed his jacket off the sofa piled with shipping boxes he had yet to open. It was only two days until Christmas and he hadn't wrapped one damned thing. He was tempted to pay Melanie and Jodi to come over and wrap them for him, but the girls couldn't keep a secret to save their lives, and they would see their own gifts ahead of time. He would have to sit down this evening and wrap them himself. Or better yet, put a bow and a tag on the boxes and call it a day.

He threw on his jacket and picked up a bucket of one of Gran's nifty pecan picker uppers. Gran's trees were still dropping a few pecans, and if he could find enough, his mother promised to bake a pecan pie. The cold wind off the lake ruffled his hair, but the winter sun shone brightly and the water sparkled. He had gathered up almost half a bucket of pecans, when Oscar drove up in the golf cart with two fishing poles and a couple buckets.

"Dad said you had to drive the boat," he groused. "Otherwise, I have to fish off Holly's dock."

Wade shrugged nonchalantly. "Fishing's good off the dock."

"Seriously?" Oscar asked indignantly.

Wade's face split into a wicked grin. "*Gotcha*. Of course we'll take the boat, doofus. Is that spot up by the falls still good?"

"As far as I know." He handed Wade a set of keys attached to a floater. Wade put the bucket and the picker-upper on Gran's front porch and hopped in the golf cart beside Oscar. Russ's boat was housed in a floating dock on an artificial peninsula sticking out in the lake.

"You ever seen what the boat launch ramp and the peninsula look like from a drone?" Oscar asked as he and Wade carried the poles and the bait bucket to the boat.

Wade rolled his eyes. "Like Big Jim and the twins. I guess your generation would call it junk."

"Just checkin'." Oscar's grin was cheeky.

They untied the boat and clambered in. It took Wade three tries to get the engine going, then they headed up the back side of the lake toward the picturesque falls that fell from the Verde Vineyard property. They passed Jack Briscoe's dock, where a couple of school-aged boys were dangling fishing poles in the water. The lake narrowed and tall limestone cliffs thrust upward from the water's edge. The wind seemed colder in the fast-moving boat, and Wade's ears were numb and his lips tingling by the time they rounded the curve leading to the falls.

He slowed down until they reached the spot where they'd had luck in the past. Oscar threw the anchor and they baited their hooks. Wade cast his line and began the slow, painstaking process of reeling the bait through the water. Oscar threw out his line in the opposite direction. He wasn't quite as good at it as Wade, but it flew a respectable distance before plopping in the water.

They fished in companionable silence for a few minutes. "Is Mom geared up for the big party tomorrow?" Wade asked as he cast his line again. It had become a tradition for her and Russ to hold an open house at the vineyard on Christmas Eve. Everyone in Heaven's Point and Verde was invited, and nearly everybody came to enjoy Christmas treats and Verde Vineyard's finest wines.

"Yep. She said she was, anyway. I hope she's still not upset tomorrow at the party. She and Dad weren't too thrilled when Denton showed up this morning." Oscar slowly reeled his line through the water.

Wade froze. Had Denton somehow found out about him and given his mother hell about it? "What did he want?" he asked through stiff lips.

Oscar blew out a breath. "It seems my sperm donor's out of prison now. He told his PO that he was looking to find me. The PO told the San Antonio cops and they called the Verde County sheriff. Denton came out to tell Dad and Mom to call the sheriff if the asswipe shows his face. Dad said something and Denton reminded him he wasn't a deputy anymore and to let the guys who still wore their badges take care of him." Oscar grinned. "Pissed Dad off thoroughly."

"Denton does that by breathing." He looked at Oscar, worried. "Do they really think he'll find you? Do they really think he'll show?"

Oscar shrugged. "I doubt it. He never cared jack-shit about me before. He's the kind who says crap to get everybody riled up. I told that to Mom and Dad. It made Dad feel a little better. Mom's still freaked."

"She would be. After all the shit my birth family put her through." He looked at Oscar. "How would you feel if he did show up?"

"Wouldn't give a damn one way or another. He's out of my life." Oscar cast his line again.

"He's still your father. He's still your blood kin."

Oscar turned around and looked at Wade with narrowed eyes. "Like hell he's still my father. That blood kin bit don't mean shit."

It was Wade's turn to stare. "You don't think it matters?"

Oscar shook his head. "Not one damned bit. It's only DNA."

"I don't get it."

"So I hear."

Wade's eyes widened. "Mom talked to you?"

Oscar rolled his eyes. "No. But I've overheard a few things maybe I wasn't supposed to." His trademark snark disappeared and he looked at Wade solemnly. "This is how it is for me: my sperm donor, and my egg-maker. They weren't good people. They were shits, if you want to know the truth. They drank and they did drugs and they didn't take care of us. I didn't know it at the time, but the luckiest night of my life was when your lover and his partner found us in that trailer park. I got lucky again a few months later, when these really nice people showed up at the children's home where we were staying. They were willing to take me and my sisters home with them. They wanted to take care of me. For the first time in my life, I didn't have to steal food to eat." He stopped and wiped his eyes. "They wanted to give me their *name*." He looked at Wade defiantly. "Who do you think are my parents? The asswipes where I got my DNA, or the people who love me?"

Wade looked across the boat at Oscar. "It was that simple for you."

"No, it wasn't simple at all." Oscar smiled faintly. "I had to learn a few things. The therapist in Austin helped. As much as Mom and Dad had to pay her, she better have helped at least some. But you know what really sealed the deal for me? It was the talk Gramps had with me the last time I got caught stealing diapers at the grocery store. He explained that I was a Riley now and that Rileys don't do things like that. He said it was time for me to start acting like a Riley." He grinned wickedly. "I hope he meant it. I've heard rumors about Dad and Gramps when they were younger."

"I doubt he meant you to take it that far," Wade said dryly.

Oscar's grin faded. "But he was right. I think it was that afternoon when it finally sank in. Russ and Angie Riley are my parents. I choose *them*. I want to be like *them*. I'm gonna act the way they act. DNA's not worth shit in my book."

He looked at Wade with eyes that blazed. "It doesn't have to be in yours. Damn it, Wade. I don't know why you even give a shit about the Baxter DNA. Angie Riley's your mother and she's been your mother since you were six years old. The Riley family took you in and consider you their own. Choose her. Be like the Rileys. Not the Baxters."

Wade's pole bobbed in the water and he started turning his reel. "Wow, get a load of this sucker. It's a big one."

***

Choose her. Be like the Rileys. Not the Baxters.

Could it be that simple?

Wade sat in the middle of the living room floor, opening the shipping boxes. His mom had fried up the bucket of fish he and Oscar caught, and then he'd spent a couple hours pitching in setting up for the party held in the tasting room, which doubled as an event center and wedding venue.

His partially healed incision limited his ability to haul tables and move chairs, but he and Melanie discovered they shared a talent for spreading out tablecloths and placing poinsettia centerpieces in the perfect spot. It was after eleven before he got back to the cottage. It was just as well that he had something to do this evening. He wasn't going to sleep much tonight. Not with the thoughts churning inside his head.

His talk with Oscar had been thought-provoking.

The kid was right. It was all a matter of choice.

Buck Baxter had chosen to drink and beat on his wife. He had chosen to cheat on Angie with an under-aged girl. He had chosen to pick up his ten-year-old son and throw him into a brick wall.

Molly Baxter had chosen to destroy his mother's business. She had chosen to point a gun at her own grandson. She had chosen to pull the trigger. She had chosen to take her own life.

Denton Baxter chose to be a homophobe and a racist. Abel Baxter chose to drink and be an asshole.

Angie Baxter chose to love her stepson as her own. She chose to stay in an abusive relationship to protect him from his father. She chose to adopt him. She chose to take a bullet meant for him.

The Riley family chose to love him like he was their own.

Angie and Russ Riley chose to adopt three more children and lavish them with love.

Oscar Riley chose to be like the parents who loved him.

It was absolutely, positively, entirely a matter of choice.

Wade had a choice as well. He could choose to remain a Baxter in his mind. He could choose to think himself ugly like the rest of them. He could continue to believe that his being gay was ugly, because that's what the Baxters believed. He could continue to let Benny's contempt haunt him. He could continue to despise himself for who and what he was.

Or he could choose to listen to his mother and Russ.

Mom believed he was the best of the best. Russ thought he was a fine man. Neither of them thought a thing about him being gay. Emily and Jason were good with who he was. So were his friends at the Durango. Maybe it was time to listen to them for a change. Maybe it was time to start thinking of himself as good. Maybe it was time to realize that being gay wasn't ugly at all. It was perfectly all right.

Maybe it was time to start loving himself a little.

That would be easier said than done. He had a lot of negative feelings to work through. It would be a long time before he would be able to accept himself completely, the way Owen did. But at least he was ready to make a start.

He bit his lip. He didn't know whether to talk to Owen or not. It would be a long time before he would really have his head on straight.

Owen might not be willing to wait for him.

All he could do was ask.

He would talk to Owen when he got back to San Antonio.

***

Wade pulled the gaudy Christmas sweater over his head and smoothed it down over his dress shirt and tie. Why his mother insisted on making him and the kids dress up for this, he had no idea. But if she wanted him looking fancy, he'd do it. He ran a comb through his hair. It was early yet for his mother's party, but if he arrived ahead of time he could add his gifts to the already ridiculously huge pile under the Christmas tree.

He sat on the bed and tugged on a boot and smoothed down his brand-new starched jeans. He was pulling on the other one when the doorbell rang. Probably one of his elderly neighbors hoping to catch a ride with him to the party. He would have to shove the Christmas presents stashed in his backseat over a little, but he could take a couple of people with him.

He stomped down in his boot and headed for the front door. He stood in shock at the sight of Owen on the other side of the screen, his hands in the pockets of an overcoat and a hopeful expression on his face. He looked at Wade's dress shirt and tie and his face fell. "Have I come at a bad time?" he asked uncertainly.

"No, not at all. Come in."

What's Owen doing here?

Wade unlatched the door and moved aside to let him enter. He drank in the sight of the man he'd missed so badly. Owen looked good. Really good. Like life finally agreed with him.

It was a look he wore well.

"May I take your coat? Are you thirsty? Can I get you a soda?"

"I'm fine. But I need to talk to you." Owen handed over his coat. He wore a black turtleneck sweater that showed off his broad shoulders and chest. It was all Wade could do not to reach out and touch him. Instead, he hung the coat over a dining room chair and pointed toward the living room.

Owen sat on the sofa and patted the cushion next to him. "No, over here," he said when Wade moved to a chair. "I've got some things to say to you that are going to be hard to get out and I want to be holding your hand while I say them."

Wade blinked as despair washed over him. "If you're going to break it off with me entirely, you can do it from across the room."

Owen's lips quirked up. "Actually, I was going to confess to being an ass and beg you to take me back. Now can you please come a little closer?"

Wade smiled. "For that, sure."

He sat beside Owen.

Owen picked up his hand and kissed it. "I had a hard time convincing your mother to tell me where you were. It seems she took exception to me treating you the way I did."

Wade winced. "Sorry."

"Russ changed her mind. Reminded her that I'm a man and I can't help being a jerk on occasion. Although he did add that if I hurt you again, he had some pruning shears that would have me singing soprano."

"Ouch. Sorry they fussed at you."

"Oh, hell. That's nothing compared to the ass-chewing I got from Letti. That woman tore into me like I've never been torn into before. Ripped me a new one up one side and down the other."

"Why?"

"I told her what happened between us. She was furious. Said I was self-absorbed, self-centered, and a jerk. And she was right." He turned to Wade, a solemn expression on his face. "I'm sorry. I acted like a complete ass and I let you down." He gripped Wade's hand. "She told me I needed to love you and accept you whether you accepted yourself or not. She said I needed to be there for you." A tear slipped from his eye and ran down his cheek. "I want to do that. Be there for you. Love you. Accept you. Are you willing to let me do that? Or is it too late for us?"

"No, it's not too late." Wade leaned forward and gave Owen a tender kiss. "I was going to try to talk to you after Christmas. See if there was any hope for us. Or if you wanted to move on."

"Why would I want to move on?"

"Because it's going to take me some time to get my head on straight. I may have sort of gotten started, but it won't be quick and easy."

"What kind of start have you gotten?"

"It was a talk I had with Oscar yesterday in the fishing boat. You know his backstory."

"Enough of it."

"Well. I said something about his birth father and how Oscar carried his blood and was informed in no uncertain terms that DNA doesn't matter one damn bit to my little brother. Russ and Angie Riley are Oscar's parents and I better not forget it. He chooses them as his family and he chooses to be like them. Not the lowlifes he shares DNA with."

"Smart kid."

"He said I needed to do the same. He said Angie was my mother and had been since I was little, and that I needed to choose to be like her, not the Baxters. I need to realize the Baxter DNA doesn't matter."

"You're already like her and not them. You're nothing like the assholes I met. Or the dead ones."

"I need to start believing it." He squeezed Owen's hand. "That's the hard part. Really and truly believing it. And believing it's all right to be gay. Mom and Russ have sort of known for a long time. They don't care. They love me. So do Emily and Jason. So do my friends at the Durango. So do you."

"Yeah, I do."

"I need to learn to be okay with being who I am along with the rest of you. That's not going to happen overnight."

"I know. That's where I come in. With the love and support you need. And some wild sex."

"There'll be plenty of wild sex. I promise." He leaned forward and captured Owen's lips with his own.

Their kiss was long and lingering, and oh so sweet, filled with all the love they could pour into it. Wade held his lover in his arms as Owen's lips and his touch promised a future of warmth and love and laughter. And passion, he thought as Wade's cock began to harden. He could hear Owen's breath catch in his throat as he ran his hands down Wade's back.

"Damn, we better stop before we can't," Wade said against Owen's lips.

"Oh my God. You're not healed yet. I'm so sorry."

"It's not that. I'm healed up fine and will be delighted to demonstrate that to you, interesting scar and all, later this evening. Mom's party starts in a few minutes and I don't want to be late."

"That's all right. I figured you don't answer your emails in a dress shirt and tie. Take your time. I'll be okay here while you're gone."

Wade took a deep breath. It was time. If he was going to believe that gay was not ugly, not something to be hidden, and that he was not ugly, he was going to have to start living like he believed it. "I have a better idea. Come with me."

Owen looked startled. "Are you sure? That's a mighty big step."

"Yeah, it is. Maybe it's time to give the people of Heaven's Point and Verde the chance to love the real Wade Baxter."

"If you're sure."

"I'm sure."

He gave Owen his coat and put on his own. The sun shone brightly as they barreled down the narrow ranch road that led to the vineyard. His heart pounded in his throat as he drove through the gates and into the parking lot, jammed with dust-covered cars and trucks. They got out of the truck and Wade grasped Owen's hand tightly in his own. He trembled only a little as they walked together across the lot and into the big, airy tasting room adorned with Christmas lights, wreaths, poinsettias, and a big Christmas tree.

Wade stopped in the door and looked around. In one corner, his old football coach Jack Briscoe stood next to his doctor wife and juggled a plate of Christmas treats. Russ's sister, Holly, and her husband, Jimmy, chatted with Gran and Gramps. Judge Riley was having a lively discussion of some sort with Betty and Joe Bob Cleburne. Cathy Flores chased a toddler across the room on her prosthetic leg. Tommy Joe Reece sat at a table in his wheelchair with his pregnant wife on his lap. Wade spotted other folks, friends from his past, some of whom he'd known since first grade.

They were all here.

He and Owen stood for a minute as the crowd spotted the two of them and grew quiet.

Owen squeezed his hand. His mother gave them a warm smile from the buffet line. Russ gave them a thumbs-up from behind the bar.

"Hello, everybody," Wade called out, his voice carrying to every corner of the room. "I'd like you to meet Owen Aldrete."

EPILOGUE

Jessica Clary sat back in her chair and fought not to roll her eyes. Loretta Castillo leaned forward in the chair, her expression earnest. "I really think Jeremy would make a wonderful Curly, don't you? He has so much talent. It honestly takes my breath away."

"He's talented, yes," Jessica conceded to Jeremy's mother. "And I look forward to seeing him in major roles in the future. But he's only been with us for six months. And Curly's a bit of a big role for a six-year-old. Just think of all those lines he'd have to memorize. So no, I don't think we'll be using Jeremy for Curly."

Loretta's face fell. "He's going to be so disappointed."

No, Mama Castillo was the one who was going to be disappointed. Jeremy wasn't going to care one way or another. "Actually, Jeremy seemed excited to be dancing in the ensemble. And of course, he'll be right on the front row. He's an excellent dancer, and we'll want to take advantage of that."

Loretta perked right up. "He is, isn't he? So he'll be on the front row. That's good."

"And later, when he has more experience, he'll certainly be in the running for lead roles. He's quite talented."

"Well, if you're sure."

"I'm positive." Jessica smiled encouragingly.

She sang Jeremy's praises for a couple more minutes, and with a sigh of relief, showed Loretta Castillo to the door.

There were days being the Children's Academy Director sucked, and today was one of those days. She shook her head and counted on her fingers. Loretta was the fifth parent today she'd had to soothe. As much as she appreciated the support the Durango parents offered, too often that support came with a boatload of unrealistic expectations, like Loretta believing that a six-year-old could carry the lead in a full-length stage play. Well, almost full length. The elementary productions were shorter than the teenage and adult shows. But most of the time it still took a nine or ten-year-old to pull off the leads. At least Loretta had been polite. Letti Aldrete as of late had become the stage parent from hell, and Jessica was thoroughly sick and tired of the pushy woman.

She left the door to her office open and sat with a printout of their current budget. Thank God for the Harrington Grant and the Navarro Corporation's generosity. Between their largesse and the tuition their more affluent parents paid, the Academy budget was healthy. But she had a teacher shortage at the moment. True love had cost her two of her instructors when they moved out of town with their boyfriends. A third lost her day job in San Antonio and had taken another one in Dallas. Her other instructors were covering some of the scheduled classes, and she and Rachel were covering the rest. But she needed to find new instructors, and soon. The parents who were paying expected top-of-the-line instruction for their children. Jessica was determined that they get the quality they were paying for.

She put the budget printout aside and was going through a bunch of lackluster resumes in her email when she looked up to see one of her favorite people peeking around the corner with a smile on his face.

"Wade. You're back." She jumped up and enveloped him in a huge hug. "Are you all better now?"

Wade hugged her back. "They decided on another damn round of antibiotics, but I finish those in a couple of days. I went back to work yesterday, and I'm dancing enough to audition for *Oklahoma.*"

"That's super. Is Owen auditioning also?"

"Yep. And I brought someone with me today that I hope will also grace us with an audition. Brian, come meet Jessica Clary, our Academy Director, and one of our most talented actresses, when we can pry her loose from her Academy responsibilities."

Wade moved aside and his companion stepped forward. Jessica's eyes widened as the newcomer came into view. *Oh. Wow.* Six feet of sexy male stood in front of her. Broad shoulders. Muscled chest. Narrow waist. Square jaw. Sexy dimples. Dancing green eyes. And the reddest hair she'd ever seen, that hadn't come out of a bottle. What a looker.

And, dammit, probably gay if he was a good friend of Wade's. Jessica tamped down her enthusiasm. Still, the man was worth a fantasy or two, if nothing else.

"Jessica, this is Brian Howard. He and I did a little theater together at A and M. He's the one who dragged me to my first audition and got me started in the theater, at College Station. I'm hoping to return the favor."

"Glad to meet you," she murmured.

Brian's eyes widened and he took her hand. "Well, hello there. I am so glad to meet you. Wade, you didn't tell me the Academy director was young and gorgeous. I was thinking more a forty-year-old schoolmarm." His fingers trailed over hers for a moment as he gave her a once-over.

She was glad she wasn't dressed in her usual yoga pants and loose t-shirt, having opted this morning for figure-hugging skinny jeans and a lacy camisole.

"No. Twenty-five and as beautiful as they come," Wade said. "She works magic on stage, with the kids."

"I don't know I'd call it magic," she protested, "but the kids frequently surprise us with their talent. So you're an old college buddy of Wade's?"

"We had a class together. I said something about doing a show, and Wade mentioned that he'd done a production or two in high school. So my girlfriend and I shanghaied him. Wouldn't take no for an answer."

"And aren't we glad," Jessica said. "So will you be joining us for auditions Sunday?"

"Based on the warm reception I've gotten from everyone this afternoon, that would be most likely." He gave her a sexy smile and another appreciative once-over before disappearing with Wade.

Jessica sat down in her chair with a thump. Well, that was interesting. Brian Howard was one good-looking tall drink of water. That smile would have every woman at the Durango hyperventilating. He must be talented or Wade wouldn't be trying to recruit him. And from the way he was checking her out and flirting with her, he didn't have a gay bone in his body.

He was an Aggie. A graduate of Texas A&M. Other than the members of the Corps of Cadets who went into the military, A&M was known for cranking out farmers, veterinarians, and engineers.

Brian was most likely an engineer like Wade. He didn't get up in the morning and strap on a holster with a pistol. He didn't get involved with hostage situations or chase down criminals or defuse bombs. He made his living in a perfectly safe manner, building bridges and the like. His loved ones didn't have to sweat blood every time he left to go to work.

He would be the perfect boyfriend.

She sure hoped he asked her out on a date.

ABOUT THE AUTHOR

The author of over thirty romance novels, Emily Mims combined her writing career with a career in public education until leaving the classroom to write full time. The mother of two sons, she and her husband split their time between central Texas, eastern Tennessee, and Georgia visiting their kids and grandchildren. For relaxation Emily plays the piano, organ, dulcimer, and ukulele for two different performing groups, and even sings a little. She says, "I love to write romances because I believe in them. Romance happened to me and it can happen to any woman—if she'll just let it."

Connect with Emily:

facebook.com/emily.mims.756

twitter.com/emilymimsauthor

instagram.com/mims_emily

website: emilymims.com

www.BOROUGHSPUBLISHINGGROUP.com

If you enjoyed this book, please write a review. Our authors appreciate the feedback, and it helps future readers find books they love. We welcome your comments and invite you to send them to info@boroughspublishinggroup.com. Follow us on Facebook, Twitter and Instagram, and be sure to sign up for our newsletter for surprises and new releases from your favorite authors.

Are you an aspiring writer? Check out www.boroughspublishinggroup.com/submit and see if we can help you make your dreams come true.